DEDICATION

For Richard and Maureen Lee
Special friends.

Fenella-Jane Miller lives in an ancient cottage in acres of Essex woodland near Colchester with her husband. She has two grown-up children and two grandchildren. Her other novels include *The House Party*, *A Debt of Honour* and *A Suitable Husband*.

For more information visit:
www.fenellajanemiller.co.uk

TWO GENTLEMEN FROM LONDON

When Colonel Robert Sinclair and his friend Major Simon Dudley arrive unannounced, Annabel Bentley is greatly displeased. She and her mother, Lady Sophia, have been hiding from her stepfather, Sir Randolph Rushton, for years — and Rushton is well-known to the colonel. Now it's only a matter of time before their whereabouts is revealed and Rushton arrives to snatch them back ... unless the two gentlemen from London prove to be more than chance acquaintances ...

Books by Fenella-Jane Miller
Published by The House of Ulverscroft:

THE UNCONVENTIONAL MISS WALTERS
A SUITABLE HUSBAND
A DISSEMBLER
THE MÉSALLIANCE
LORD THURSTON'S CHALLENGE
A DEBT OF HONOUR
THE HOUSE PARTY
THE GHOSTS OF NEDDINGFIELD HALL

FENELLA-JANE MILLER

TWO GENTLEMEN FROM LONDON

Complete and Unabridged

ULVERSCROFT
Leicester

First published in Great Britain in 2009 by
Robert Hale Limited
London

First Large Print Edition
published 2010
by arrangement with
Robert Hale Limited
London

British Library CIP Data

Miller, Fenella-Jane.
    Two gentlemen from London.
    1. Great Britain- -Social conditions- -Fiction.
    2. Large type books.
    I. Title
    823.9′2–dc22

    ISBN 978–1–44480–483–6   20292711

Published by
F. A. Thorpe (Publishing)
Anstey, Leicestershire

Set by Words & Graphics Ltd.
Anstey, Leicestershire
Printed and bound in Great Britain by
T. J. International Ltd., Padstow, Cornwall

This book is printed on acid-free paper

1

'Miss Bentley, lawks a mussy! They're here. Young Fred saw the carriage turn into the lane not ten minutes ago.'

Annabel Bentley dropped the jar of bramble jelly she had been about to place on the shelf in the pantry. 'After so long? I had thought Mama and I safe from him.' Stepping over the sweet mess on the flagstones she gathered up her skirts, calling over her shoulder as she ran. 'You and Tom know what to do; we have about thirty minutes before they arrive.'

How had he found them? They had been so careful these past years, had not even attended church or visited Ipswich them- selves. Her heart pounding, she ran upstairs calling her mother.

'Mama, we are discovered. We must get organized, or it will be too late.' She had hoped never to be reminded of that black time again.

Lady Sophia appeared from the south facing chamber she used for her studio. As usual she had paint streaks on her face and fingers. 'Are you quite certain, my love? I can hardly credit that monster has been able to find us.'

'Well, he has. Mary and Tom are putting on the holland covers, we have to clear your studio.'

In the beginning they had practised this exercise several times, but, as the months and then the years slipped by, they had stopped rehearsing. However, the boxes were ready and it was the work of moments to fill them with the paraphernalia.

'Quickly, open the panel and I'll start taking things through.' Annabel tried to recall how long it was since she had checked their intended hiding place. It must be almost a year; the two secret rooms would be dust covered, but it was too late to worry about that. There was the clatter of footsteps and their servants arrived to disguise the bedchambers they had been occupying with covers.

'Miss Bentley, everything's ready downstairs and we shall have your rooms done in a trice. Fred is moving the horses. I reckon we'll be prepared in good time.'

'This room is finished; all we need is sufficient food and water for today and tomorrow. No doubt you will be obliged to offer accommodation tonight, but when he finds he's mistaken, he will surely leave first thing.'

'He'll not get a meal he'll enjoy tonight, I'll make sure of that.'

'Thank you, Mary. I cannot imagine why the three of you have stayed with us so long in this isolated place, but we could not have managed without you.'

'Bless you, miss, it's been our pleasure. You mustn't worry. If you and Lady Sophia get settled, we'll be up with what you need as soon as we've done here.'

Annabel stepped into the hidden passageway, relieved to see her mother had not been idle, the sconces were burning and she had sufficient illumination to fasten the panel behind her and to pick up one of the remaining boxes.

The passageways and narrow staircase led from top to bottom of the ancient mansion. The place had once been used by smugglers and although the exit to the beach had fallen into disuse years ago, it was still possible to get from the kitchen to the hidden apartment in the attic.

She followed the twists and turns without hesitation, it was so fixed in her mind. She could hear her mother moving about ahead of her and guessed she would be setting up her easel.

'There you are, my love. I shall run back and fetch the last box whilst you check we have everything we need up here. I fear the bed linen will be damp after so long.'

Annabel didn't bother to argue that she was younger and fitter and should be the one to go, for it would be untrue. Her mother was barely eight and thirty, and she nineteen on her last name day, they would be taken for sisters if ever they appeared together in public.

These secret rooms had been constructed when the house was built. There was no way to enter them via the attics, the only panels that opened were in the room that had been used as a studio and the boot room in the basement. She walked across to the low doors that opened on to the roof.

She pulled them back and stepped out, knowing she could not be seen from below. Brandon Hall, originally built in the reign of Queen Elizabeth, now had a false edifice making it appear what it was not. Behind the frontage, hidden between two chimney breasts, was a space more than large enough to walk about. She carefully removed the brick that filled the peephole.

Her throat constricted and her hands clenched. Fred had not been mistaken. Already halfway down the long curving drive was a smart, black travelling carriage. They had not received a visitor since they had joined Great-Aunt Beth as nobody knew they were there. It could only be her stepfather, Randolph Rushton, and his loathsome man of affairs.

A vivid flash of lightning split the sky. She counted, had reached five when the thunder followed. The storm they had been anticipating all day would be upon them within the hour. She prayed the river that ran parallel to the lane would not flood; the last time it had done so it had been a week before the road was passable.

Her mother appeared at the door, her face pinched and pale. 'Come in, my dear, we must get ourselves settled whilst there's still light enough to do so. You know we cannot risk more than a single candle once it is dark.'

'Very well, Mama. The carriage will be here imminently. We can't move about once it arrives; you know how sound echoes down the passageway.'

★　★　★

The coach rocked violently. 'God's teeth! Sinclair, are you certain we have taken the correct turning?'

Colonel Robert Sinclair grinned at his companion. 'The yokel the coachman questioned a while ago directed us along this

5

godforsaken track. It's your family we're visiting, Dudley, not mine, remember.'

'My sister said she lives in rural splendour, not that she lived somewhere as inaccessible as this.'

The horses slowed to a walk and Robert lowered the window. 'I can see something carved into the gatepost.' He leant out and could just make out some letters under the verdigris. 'Yes, it's definitely Brandon Manor.' He shouted up to the coachman. The groom sitting next to him on the box, hung precariously over the edge to listen. 'This is it. The drive is in no better state than the lane. Take it carefully, I don't want my horses lamed.'

'Very well, Colonel, we'll take it steady.'

The driver waved his whip in acknowledgement and Robert resumed his place on the squabs. This was turning out to be a more interesting excursion than he'd anticipated. When Dudley had suggested a visit to darkest Suffolk to see his sister Amelia, he had agreed. Since Waterloo, and reduced to half pay, even a sojourn in the country seemed preferable to kicking his heels in Town, and having too much time to dwell on his loss.

'I know your sister has been widowed, but surely her finances are not so parlous that the estate has fallen into disrepair?'

6

'To tell you the truth, I know little about Brandon Manor, or her dead husband. She met and married Sir George Barton whilst I was in the Peninsular with you fighting Napoleon. She has two children, I misremember their names, but from what I recall, Barton was a young man with deep pockets. Amelia wouldn't have looked at him otherwise.'

Robert smiled. 'She always said she would marry money; but I'm surprised she chose someone who lives so remotely. I doubt she has much social life stuck out here in the back of beyond.'

The sky was rent by a sheet of lightning closely followed by the rumble of thunder. 'That's all we need, a storm. The going is too poor for us to make faster progress; I fear we're going to be caught in a downpour.'

'At least we will be well looked after when we arrive. Amelia keeps a good table. This journey has been beyond tedious, I cannot wait to stretch my legs and enjoy a decent meal.' Simon Dudley shuddered. 'The repast we were given last night beggars belief.'

'It didn't prevent you from finishing it,' Robert said drily. The carriage dropped into another pothole tilting dangerously; he was catapulted from his seat. 'Dammit! That's the axle gone. God knows how we're going to get it fixed out here.'

He untangled himself from his friend and reached up to grasp the door which was now above his head. 'Did I hurt you?' Major Dudley shook his head. 'I must get out and help Jethro with the horses. We're still a mile from the house; I fear we're going to have to walk.'

The team might be in imminent danger of entangling themselves in the traces. He prided himself on having four incomparable matched bays and had no intention of letting any one of them become injured. Heaving himself upright, he smashed the door open and thrust through the opening to roll down the carriage to the ground.

His driver was before him and had his knife out to slice through the leather. There was no sign of the groom. He ran to take hold of the bit of the lead horse, he pulled the animal's head down and spoke soothingly until it calmed. 'Where's Billy?'

'I ain't had time to look, sir. He went over the side and I've not seen him since.'

There was the thump of boots as they hit the ground behind him. 'Dudley, my groom's hurt. Check on him.' He knew his friend wouldn't question his orders; after all he'd been following his commands during the years they had served together in the same regiment.

'A concussion; he's out cold, but his pulse's steady. How the devil are we going to get him to the house?'

'I can see help arriving; there's a pony and trap heading this way. I find it decidedly odd that Amelia can provide us with nothing better than that.'

Dudley shrugged. 'I suppose it might have been sensible to have informed her of our coming.'

'Good God! How did the regiment survive with you in charge of transport? I should not have agreed to accompany you, or use my carriage, if I had known we were not expected.'

The trap clattered to a halt beside them and an elderly retainer scrambled out, a younger version, obviously his son, close behind. 'It's going to rain something heavy any time now, sir, so we best get you to the hall before it do.'

Robert nodded. 'My groom is injured, take him and our bags. Major Dudley and myself will ride.' The man touched his cap and vanished to the far side of the tilted carriage to collect the patient. He was about to swing up on the horse he was holding when something the man had said made him stop.

'Is this Brandon Manor?'

The two servants staggered around, the comatose body between them. The older man answered. 'Bless you, sir, no it ain't. This is Brandon Hall. Brandon Manor is ten miles away, at Upper Brandon. This here place is Lower Brandon.'

★ ★ ★

'My goodness! The coach has had a mishap.' Annabel remained with her eyes fixed to the aperture in the wall. 'The poor groom has taken a tumble from the box and he hasn't regained his feet.'

'Can you see Rushton or that obnoxious Hughes?'

'No, Mama. Just a moment, someone is emerging from the door. Thank God! It's definitely not them, even from this distance I can see this man is a head taller and far broader than either of *them*. Another has just climbed out, and he is as tall as the first.'

'Then who in the world can it be? We have received no visitors since we arrived here three and a half years ago. I cannot imagine why anyone should come by chance.'

Her mother trembled at her side and she turned to comfort her. 'I know we don't want anyone here, but it's far better than we

10

thought. If it's not your husband come to claim you back, then it's possible we are not discovered.' She placed her arm around her mother's shoulders and guided her inside. 'I shall run down and tell Mary to expect strangers. Unfortunately the broken axle will mean they are marooned here until Tom and Fred can fix it.'

She ducked into the chamber just as the skies opened. The door banged. Hastily she grabbed it, fastening it behind her. Whoever these visitors were, they could not afford to be seen by them. A casual mention by either of the unwelcome guests might somehow filter back to her stepfather.

'Why don't you light the fire, Mama? It will make the room more cheerful, and the smoke will emerge from the same stack as the one downstairs so it will not reveal our presence here.'

She arrived in the kitchen to discover Mary was about to come up with their tray. 'I have news for you. It's not Sir Randolph arriving, it is two strangers and their carriage has lost a wheel. Their groom took a fall and will need to be accommodated inside where you can take care of him.'

'Whatever next? Shall I make them a decent supper?'

'Yes, but remember it is just as vital *they* do

11

not know we are here. I fear they might be here for a week at least, especially if the river floods.'

★   ★   ★

The tray was awkward to carry up the narrow stairs but she wouldn't dream of asking Mary to do something she wasn't prepared to do herself. Her mother had taken her advice and the fire was burning merrily. 'Here we are, there's enough food to last us until tomorrow night at least.' Carefully placing the tray on the small table by the wall she smiled. 'I must go back and collect fresh water for washing, I shall not be long.'

It was only as she returned a second time with the jug of hot water that she realized she had made a grave error by telling Mary who was expected. She prayed, whoever the gentleman were, they were not sufficiently interested to think too closely about the fact that the housekeeper knew their groom was injured. If they did, they would know at once there must be somebody else on the premises who had been watching from an upstairs window.

2

Major Dudley smiled ruefully. 'We are hopelessly astray. I'm not sure which of us is at fault here. I misheard the local and you misread the sign.'

'But, my friend, when I did *that* we were already here. It's too late to repine, we'd better get the beasts to the stable before the heavens open.'

Robert vaulted on to the back of the gelding he was holding, he was as much at home bareback as in a saddle. His friend would follow on and the coachman could bring the spare horses. The grass that ran either side of the drive was overlong, the flock of sheep he could see grazing in the distance obviously not large enough to keep it well groomed. However it was safer than the potholed drive; he kicked the animal into a canter, the pony cart trundling behind.

He called across to the elderly man, 'Are the stables at the back?'

The older man gestured to a brick archway to one side of the ancient pile. Robert wasn't fooled for a minute, the façade and windows might be modern, but he was certain the building behind was hundreds of years old. He slowed his mount to a walk and crunched under the archway into a well-swept cobbled yard. Whoever lived here, they had horses, the boxes were painted, everything spruced up as it should be.

He dismounted, waiting for the others to arrive. 'There are half-a-dozen boxes with fresh straw, I'll put Sinbad in for you, Jethro.'

'Thank you, Colonel, they'll be snug enough here all right. No worries about that.'

By the time he emerged from the loose box the pony cart had arrived at the back door; an elderly lady, her hair pinned under a crisp white cap, appeared in the doorway. 'I have a room prepared, sir, my Tom and Fred can carry the poor young man straight in.'

He frowned. How the devil did the housekeeper know there was an injured man coming? There was something havey-cavey about all this. Still, he was an uninvited guest, it was none of his business what went on here. As long as his groom was taken care of, his horses comfortable, and he and his companion had somewhere to sleep, he had no complaints.

He waited until Dudley was ready to accompany him and then followed through the back door and into the rear of the house. As he'd suspected, it was old; the low ceilings

14

and black beams making it difficult for him to walk upright.

The housekeeper appeared from a chamber. 'I beg your pardon, sir, you should have gone in by the front door. Makes no never mind now. If you'd care to follow me, I'll show you to your chambers.'

Robert had collected his bag from the cart on the way past. He liked to travel light, he wasn't one for preening and prettifying in front of a glass, like some of his cronies. He looked around with interest as she led them through the rabbit warren of passages to the front of the house. She paused in a spacious entrance hall with galleried ceiling and shields and bits of armour hanging on the panelled walls.

'I must apologize for the state of the house, sir, the mistress and her companion are away in Bath for the winter. The house is under holland covers, but we'll soon have things ready for you.'

'I am Colonel Sinclair, this Major Dudley. As you have already realized, we've arrived by accident to this place. We have come from London and it was our intention to go to Brandon Manor, at Upper Brandon, but here we are and, I'm afraid, here we'll have to stay until my coach has been repaired.'

The woman dipped in a brief curtsy. 'Mrs

Jamieson would be quite happy to accommo-
date you both for as long as you might
require, Colonel Sinclair. My son's a
wheelwright; he'll soon have your carriage
fixed. We're self-sufficient here, between us
we can do everything that's necessary.'

She'd led them up a wide oak staircase, but
stopped to catch her breath in the gallery.
Robert waited politely until she was ready to
continue. Eventually she halted in front of a
solid door.

'If you would care to take this chamber, sir,
your companion can have the one next door.'
She pushed open the door and immediately
began to whisk the covers off revealing
old-fashioned furniture. An enormous tester
bed dominated the room, its brocade
hangings clean, the linen obviously fresh.
Thankfully it would be long enough for him;
he was more used to sleeping with his feet
poking out at the end.

'Thank you . . . ?' He waited for her to
supply a name.

'Hopkins, Colonel. Do you not have your
man with you?'

'We're military gentlemen, Hopkins, we do
for ourselves.'

'The fire is laid, if you feel the need, please
light it. There's plenty of logs in the basket
and my Fred can fetch more if you need

them. Now, if you'll excuse me I must attend to the patient. There's only my husband, son and myself to look after everything here.' She bustled out and he heard her talking to Dudley as she showed him his room.

Tossing his bag on to the bed he strolled to the window; the room was surprisingly fresh for one that had been unoccupied for a considerable time. He frowned as several flashes of lightning rent the sky, followed immediately by a crash of thunder and torrential rain. Although it was barely mid-afternoon, it was almost dark.

The tinderbox was on the mantelshelf; he would need candles alight. Not the fire though. Having spent the past few years sleeping rough most of the time, he preferred his chamber to be cold. Opening his bag he removed his shaving gear and placed it on the wash stand. His jacket and spare britches he hung in the closet, he left his undergarments where they were. He felt no need to place things on shelves unnecessarily.

His stomach rumbled loudly. The meagre breakfast he'd eaten had been several hours ago. He hoped the housekeeper had provisions in; he'd not be comfortable if he thought he was eating the food from her own table.

Annabel paced the small chamber, anxiously waiting for news. She daren't go herself in case she was seen. Maybe Fred would find time to slip away and tell her who was downstairs and how they came to be at Brandon Hall in the first place.

'My dear girl, you will wear a hole in the carpet. Please, my love, come and sit down by the fire and read your book. If you will be still, I shall finish the sketch I started last night.'

'Mama, how can you be so sanguine? Are you not riven by curiosity about the strangers?'

'Of course I am, my love, but am happy to wait until someone comes up to inform me.'

Annabel sank on to a chair and picked up her novel as her mother had suggested. However, she did not immerse herself in it, being far too worried that her slip of the tongue would lead to their discovery. Half an hour passed, the only sounds in the room the crackling of the logs and the scratching of a pencil on paper. Then she heard steps approaching and there was a tap on the door.

'Come in, Mary, we've been waiting this age to know what's going on.'

'I've been busy, Miss Bentley, I've not had

time to come until now, what with the poor man who's banged his head, and the two gentlemen from London to take care of.'

'Well, Mary, tell us,' Annabel's mother asked. 'What kind of gentlemen are they?'

'Gracious, all those stairs will be the death of me!'

'Sit down and catch your breath. Pour her a drink of lemonade, Annabel.'

Mary collapsed on a chair, mopped her brow, took a long drink and smiled. 'They're both big gentlemen, the tallest of the two is the younger, and he's Colonel Sinclair. The older gentleman, the shorter one, mind you he's still bigger than my Tom or Fred, is Major Dudley.'

Annabel's lips twitched at Mary's convoluted explanation. 'We know they are from London, and that they are military, but why are they *here*?'

'It was all a mistake, they took the wrong turning. They had intended to go to Brandon Manor, came to Brandon Hall instead.'

'I should have thought of that, I had quite forgotten there is a property with a similar name to this, Mary.' Lady Sophia paused. 'You have only described the gentlemen in part, but I'm curious to know the details. It's so long since we have had contact with anyone, military or otherwise.'

The housekeeper wiped her brow on the edge of her apron. 'The colonel is dark haired, wears it overlong in my opinion, and dark-complexioned; you might call him swarthy, I suppose. Must be all the time he spent campaigning in foreign parts. I reckon it's hotter there. The major's fairer, they are both well spoken, and have prodigious appetites.'

'Good heavens! Have you fed them already?'

'That I have. Colonel Sinclair appeared in the kitchen asking if there was bread and cheese they could have as they'd not eaten since dawn. I was having none of that. They got that rabbit pie and vegetables from the garden, followed by baked apples with bramble sauce. They're in the back parlour, drinking brandy and quite content.'

Annabel was on her feet, her expression outraged. 'Drinking our brandy? How could you, Mary? We have only the one bottle and that's supposed to be for medicinal purposes.'

'I couldn't resist him, miss, he asked so handsomely. The colonel's promised to replace it, so what could I do?'

Annabel snorted her displeasure.

'My dear child, you sound like your horse. I had hoped you'd grown out of that disgusting habit.'

'I have, really, Mama. I apologize, Mary. You're right; you must behave as though neither of us are here. Take no notice of me, you know I hate to be cooped up. It makes me tetchy.'

After Mary had gone she decided the talk of food had made her hungry. The house-keeper had done them proud, apart from fresh bread, cheese, scones and plum cake, there were also meat pasties, tomatoes and salad leaves and a bowl of apples.

'Mama, there's enough here to feed us for a week. Unless, of course, the mice don't eat it first.'

Her mother was distracted and didn't answer. 'The weather is worsening, Annabel. I'm sure the river will flood and then we shall be stuck with these unwanted visitors longer than it takes to mend their carriage.'

'I'm sure the rain sounds heavier up here directly under the tiles, it might not be so bad outside.'

'Do not open the shutters to look, my love, remember we cannot risk the light being seen.'

'Mama, they are hardly likely to be blowing a cloud on the terrace when it's like a monsoon out there, are they?'

Her mother smiled. 'Here, what do you think?' She held up her sketch.

Annabel took it, sighing in admiration. 'It's beautiful. I'm sure I'm not as you have portrayed me. I wish I had your talent.'

'You can play the pianoforte and sing as well as I draw, my dear. The good Lord doesn't give his gifts indiscriminately.'

'That's another thing about being imprisoned up here, I shall not be able to play the piano until those men go. Neither shall I be able to ride out. There are more blackberries to gather, and plums and apples to be picked in the orchard.'

'I should think the plums and brambles will be spoilt by the rain, so you must forget about those. Apples will keep until you're ready to pick them.'

The rain continued overnight and she slept poorly. Her mother, on the other side of the room, appeared sound asleep. Long before dawn Annabel gave up and slipped out of bed, quietly pulling on her gown, not bothering with undergarments. The house was quiet; she'd go downstairs to make herself some tea. The guest chambers were at the front of the house, the kitchen at the back.

She pushed her feet into her indoor slippers and, with a candle in one hand, skirts in the other, crept down to the kitchen. She waited before pressing the catch that would

22

release the panel in the boot room. She allowed it to slide back a little. It was as black as pitch, no noise at all. She hadn't expected there to be any, their staff would have gone to their beds long ago, their guests also. Slipping through, she checked the panel was fully closed before emerging into the corridor. The kitchen fire was still burning and the kettle had sufficient water to be pushed back over the flames. She busied herself collecting what she needed. The house was quiet. She lit several candles and, taking one, sought the privacy of the commode in a downstairs closet.

She went in the scullery to wash her hands before returning to the kitchen. She could hear the kettle was beginning to hiss. She pushed open the door and came face to face with a veritable giant, dressed only in his britches and shirt.

⋆   ⋆   ⋆

Robert's jaw dropped. Standing in front of him, more or less dressed, was the most startlingly lovely young woman he'd ever set eyes on. From her cloud of ash-blonde hair which hung in a curtain over her shoulders, to her ankles, clearly visible below the hem of her gown, she was perfection personified. She was staring at him, eyes round with horror.

He was seldom speechless, but for some reason his composure had temporarily deserted him. 'I beg your pardon. I had no idea I would find anyone here at this time of the night.'

The girl's face was losing colour and for a moment he thought she would swoon at his feet. He shot forward, but she warded him off with a raised hand.

'This is an unmitigated disaster. Which one are you, the colonel or the major?'

Feeling rather like a schoolboy caught out in a misdemeanour he grinned. 'I'm Colonel Robert Sinclair at your service, madam.' He bowed, feeling ridiculous dressed as he was. He waited for her to identify herself, but she stared frostily, not amused in any way by the situation.

'I had no idea there was anyone else in residence. The housekeeper told us the owner and her companion had left to spend the winter in Bath.' He raised an eyebrow quizzically. Still no response. Feeling slightly silly he moved away, noticing the kettle was boiling, casually picked it up and tipped it into the pot.

The girl's gasp made him slop boiling water, narrowly missing his bare feet. 'Hell!' Remembering where he was, he replaced the kettle before speaking again. 'I beg your pardon, miss, barrack-room language.'

'Your hand? Show me your hand.'

Curious he complied, holding it up for her inspection.

'There's not a mark on it. The kettle handle is red hot. I don't understand how you haven't blistered your palm.'

'I admit it was a trifle warm. But when you're fighting you don't have time to worry about such niceties. If you want to eat, want a hot drink, and there's no common soldier to make it for you, then you do it yourself. Your hands soon harden.'

She gestured towards the table. 'Shall we be seated? It's too late to pretend I'm not here, isn't it?'

Mystified, he smiled down at her. 'I have never seen anyone more obviously here than you, but I still don't know your name.'

For a moment she hesitated, then shrugged. 'I suppose I must tell you the whole. I doubt that my mother and I could have remained shut up in the attic without coming to blows.'

What the devil was she talking about? Why should her mother be shut up in the attic? Had he come to a house where a madwoman was incarcerated? Why had the housekeeper pretended everyone was away from home?

'Why don't you sit down, I shall bring the

tea across. I believe there's a plum cake in the pantry, would you like a slice?'

'No, thank you, tea is all I require.'

They were conversing as if at an afternoon tea party. They were both immodestly dressed, it was three o'clock in the morning and they were unchaperoned. As soon as the word came into his head his amusement vanished.

'I'm sorry, but whoever you are, I cannot be here with you.'

She looked at him enquiringly. 'Why ever not? It is my kitchen, you're a guest here, and I'm making a cup of tea for us both.'

'It's not correct for you to be alone with me, and especially as neither of us are properly attired.' The teapot slipped from her hand and he reached out to capture it. He instantly regretted doing so as the boiling liquid shot out of the spout and up his arm. Swearing volubly again he dropped it on the table.

'Quickly, let me put cold water on your arm.' Before he could prevent her she'd grasped his hand and was examining the red mark. This wouldn't do. She shouldn't be standing so close to him. Shouldn't be touching him.

This young woman was a complete innocent, had no more idea that she was doing anything improper than an infant. Somehow he pushed down his rising desire, forced his mind away from wanting to snatch her into his arms and kiss her delectable mouth.

'Sit down, Colonel Sinclair, before you do yourself further harm. I realize now, that you must think me immodest being in here with you. However, I don't believe you are a threat to me. You have no wish to molest me in any way, do you?' She looked at him her azure blue eyes guileless, and he drowned in their depths. He blinked. The girl was looking at him, her brow creased.

'Are you unwell, sir? You have gone rather red.'

He snatched his hand back. 'I am perfectly well, thank you.' He knew he was being abrupt, but couldn't remain so close without revealing how he felt. It was he who was being improper, not she.

★   ★   ★

The kitchen door slammed and Annabel stared at the space that had just contained the rudest man she'd ever met. The fact that he was also inordinately attractive had not escaped her attention, but it was his behaviour she was most concerned with not his appearance.

How dare he stomp off in that way? It had been her fault, of course. When he had mentioned they were unchaperoned and he not properly dressed, she had suddenly realized the indelicacy of the situation and almost dropped the teapot. The poor man caught it and been burnt in the process.

She shrugged, it was their best teapot, so was glad it hadn't smashed on the flagstones. There was no point in wasting the tea now it was made. With a cup in her hand she sat down at the table in the flickering light and tried to make sense of what had happened. She had been closeted for twenty minutes with a total stranger, he in only his britches and shirt, she in her dress and slippers and nothing else. She ran a hand through her hair, what had possessed her to leave it loose, today of all days?

And she had taken his hand — that was unforgivable. He must think her no better than a light skirt, whatever that might be. Mama had once used the term, but neglected to tell her exactly why it was so derogatory.

However one thing was certain, the cat was well and truly out of the bag. There was no point in skulking about in the attics; they might as well move back to their bedchambers and pray that the two military gentleman proved to be discreet.

The tea drunk, she trudged back upstairs trying hard to be positive; but from whichever way she viewed the situation it was her fault. No doubt her mother would be horrified that, after all their efforts, she had ruined everything because she couldn't sleep.

3

Lady Sophia was still asleep. Annabel removed her dress and slid back into bed without her mother being aware. In fact, she was fairly certain she hadn't been missed at all. Although it was still several hours to morning she couldn't settle. She rehearsed in her mind how she was going to explain that, after all the years of planning and subterfuge, a careless moment had revealed everything.

The rain continued to pour, but thankfully without the thunder and lightning that had accompanied it earlier. Even the drum of rain on the tiles failed to lull her back to sleep. She did no more than doze, her head full of the image of a dark-complexioned man with compelling navy-blue eyes: when she eventually got up again she was heavy-eyed and belligerent and stomped about the bedroom getting dressed making no concession to her mother's slumber.

'My dear girl, why are you making so much noise? This is far too early to be in such a bad temper.'

'At last, Mama. I have to speak to you.' Annabel dropped back on to her own bed and waited for her mother to push herself upright.

'Go on, my love, it must be something bad or you would not have been so kind as to rouse me in the middle of the night.'

Annabel smiled. 'It is after seven, more than time for all sensible people to be up and doing. I have been awake since two and I've done something dreadful.' She had her mother's full attention. 'I went downstairs to make myself some tea and Colonel Sinclair wandered into the kitchen and found me there.' She waited for the reproaching look, the sigh of disappointment and was surprised when her mother merely nodded.

'I guessed it was that. I woke myself, and saw that your bed was empty. But tell me, what *sort* of man is he?'

'Good grief! How can you ask that when I have put both our lives in jeopardy?'

'My dear girl, you are being overdramatical. These might be two gentleman from London, but they are military men, and hardly a threat to us. I doubt if they've heard of us or our predicament.'

She scrambled to her feet and rushed over to embrace her mother. 'I'm so sorry. I have, as usual, ignored common sense and allowed my selfishness to spoil things.'

'No, my darling, I will hear no more of it.

31

You have willingly lived in isolation with me, not once demanding to attend a ball or party or to meet other people. It is high time we rejoined society however difficult that might be.'

'But why, then, did we hide away in the attics if you were ready to reveal our whereabouts to the world?'

Her mother pushed back the covers and stood up, yawning elegantly. 'Hardly the world, my love, merely two gentlemen from London. It was after Mary described them as being young and personable that I realized it would not be right to keep you closeted away any longer.'

'I am still under age, Mama, could Sir Randolph not force me to return with him?'

Her mother's lips pursed and her eyes flashed. 'It would be over my dead body, my dear. That monster will not involve you in his sadistic practices.'

'I also think, Mama, it is time we discussed what actually took place. Sir Randolph treated you cruelly, I know that much. He did so from the first, so why did you suddenly decide we must run away?'

'It's difficult to tell you. You might be almost of age, but you are still such an innocent, not aware of the evil that can be in men's souls. Your stepfather treated me in a way no wife should have to endure. That was why I sent you away to school.'

Annabel remembered her school days perfectly. She had been far happier amongst her friends than she had been at home. Each time she returned, her mother had been thinner and with dark circles under her eyes, and even to a child it had been obvious something was badly wrong. It wasn't until she was a little older that she realized her stepfather mistreated her mother, that she was permanently bruised and injured from his degradation.

However, this didn't explain why, when Annabel had returned to the marital home on her fifteenth summer, that her mother had decided to run away. She clearly recalled the morning; Mama had been so badly beaten she was unable to rise. Sir Randolph had been at home. It was the first time he had seen his stepdaughter for several years.

She shuddered; she knew why Mother had taken her away. 'He wanted *me*? He intended to abuse me in the same way?'

There were tears glistening in her mother's eyes. 'He did, my darling. He chose me as his bride because I was still young. I married your father when I was scarcely out of the schoolroom. You were born just before my eighteenth birthday, and your papa was killed soon afterwards. I was in India, I was destitute.'

Her mother struggled for composure and Annabel went to sit beside her, taking her shaking hands in hers. 'Sir Randolph was in that country on business; his assistance was invaluable. He was everything he should be, treated me with respect, was there as protection and support. It wasn't until we were on the ship sailing home that he made his feelings clear. I didn't love him, but he was charming, and prepared to offer us both a home. The pension your father left was insufficient to keep us out of the workhouse.'

Annabel knew this to be an exaggeration. Her father had been part of the East India Company, and although there was little private income, he had come from a respectable family and his pension would have been adequate. However, her mother was the daughter of an earl — it was from him she inherited her title. Her grandfather had rejected her mother when she had eloped.

'But you were in mourning, how could you have married him so soon?'

'No one on the ship knew my circumstances. I had not gone into black, I had not the wherewithal to purchase the necessary material. You must remember, you were a

34

baby, I, only twenty. When Sir Randolph suggested we marry as soon as we docked, said he would apply for a special licence, I could see no objection. No one knew who I was, my family had washed their hands of me when I ran off with your father. They would offer me no succour, and I would not have dreamt of going to them for help.'

By this time her mother was washed and dressed and they drifted into the sitting-room. Annabel opened the shutters and viewed the gloomy prospect. The sky was still leaden, the rain draining as if from a leaky bucket.

'And so you married Sir Randolph; were you ever happy together?'

Her mother shook her head. 'As soon as the ring was on my finger he expected me to do things that I found abhorrent. My reluctance to participate in his unnatural practices earned me physical chastisement. Over the years it was beating I received, but I far preferred that to being degraded in the marriage bed.'

She had no real idea to what her mother was referring. She vaguely knew what took place between a man and woman, of course, as she had seen farmyard fowl mating. She felt a wave of nausea as she imagined what her mama might have been forced to endure.

Marriage was not something she cared to contemplate; a wife was no better than a chattel. Unbidden a pair of dark-blue eyes and a friendly smile slid into her head. What fustian! She was not going to be so easily charmed — all men were no doubt the same underneath.

'So when he turned his attention to me you decided we should join Great-aunt Beth?'

'I did, my dear. As you recall, when we arrived Aunt Beth was already bedridden. I was so glad that we came in time to be a comfort to her in her last years. Although, I own, even though it was at her insistence, I still do not feel comfortable at having persuaded Tom to bury her in the orchard without benefit of clergy.'

'But you know, Mama, if we had involved the vicar then the will would have been read, and your husband would immediately have known where we were.'

'Thank you for reminding me. But now I think it is time to be brave. You are an adult. I'm quite certain you have the fortitude to resist *his* base demands. I wish to give Aunt Beth the benefit of a funeral service.'

'Yes, but *you* are still his wife. He has the law on his side; could he not remove us both from here by force?'

'Exactly! But, my dear, do we not have two

strong military gentlemen living under our roof at this very moment? They have been sent to us in answer to my prayers.'

This was not the response she had expected, but it made a strange kind of sense. Would her mother wish to involve the colonel and his friend if she knew the full story of what had taken place last night?

'Mama, Colonel Sinclair is the rudest man I have ever met. I have no wish to be beholden to him. I think you should reconsider sharing our story with complete strangers.'

Her mother's tinkling laugh filled the attic room. 'Good heavens! I have no intention of telling them anything. I merely said whilst they are at Brandon Hall it is safe for us to mingle with them.' She smiled lovingly. 'And, my love, I don't believe you have met any other men to compare the colonel with.'

'I don't need to have a comparison, Mama, I'm quite capable of recognizing bad manners when I meet them. Anyway, there is no point in us remaining up here as Colonel Sinclair already knows we are in residence. I have no intention of *mingling* with either of the gentlemen from London, Mama, but it will be a relief not to spend further time in the attics.'

She stared at the tray of food with

disfavour. 'What about all this? I shall have to carry it back downstairs. We cannot afford to waste it.'

'No, my dear, Fred can come and collect it. Now, we must return at once to our chambers; I shall be able to wash in comfort and restore my appearance in front of a glass.'

'You know very well, Mama, that even dressed in a flour sack you would still be beautiful.'

★ ★ ★

Colonel Sinclair did not sleep again that night. He was dressed and out of his bedchamber at dawn. The house was dark and silent and he needed his candlestick to find his way to the small parlour they had occupied the previous night. He kicked a blaze from the fire then found more logs and coal to add to the flames. Since Maria had died he'd found no woman of interest, but a single meeting with this unknown girl had made him very much aware that he was a red-blooded male.

It was a filthy day; even if the housekeeper, Hopkins, was correct, and her son an expert wheelwright, it would be impossible to leave Brandon Hall until the weather improved. He rubbed his unshaven chin. Dare he risk venturing into the kitchen a second time in order to find himself water to shave?

His mouth curled as he remembered the angelic apparition he had met there last time. Breathtakingly lovely, her pale-gold hair and vivid blue eyes gave the girl the appearance of an angel. But there the resemblance ended, she was no more of angelic temperament than he was. But innocent as one, that was certainly true.

He had known there was something odd about this set-up from the first. But why in God's name had this young woman felt the need to hide in the attics with her mad mother when they arrived, he had no notion. But he intended to find out. As soon as the house was awake he would demand some answers.

He took his candle and found his way back through the labyrinth of corridors to the kitchen; there was no sign of Hopkins, or her husband and son, so he set about restoring the old-fashioned range and fetching in logs and coal. Pushing the kettle back over the flames as soon as they were hot enough, he unbolted the back door and went to check that his precious team had suffered no ill effects from yesterday's excitement.

★   ★   ★

In the comfort of her own bedchamber, Annabel quickly washed and found something fresh to put on. She viewed the result in the over-mantel mirror. The royal-blue damask suited her fair complexion, and the closely fitting waist, full skirt and snug bodice made the best of the feminine assets the good Lord had kindly given her. She was fairly sure that the garments she and her mother wore, although of good quality, were hopelessly outmoded. This had never bothered her before.

Her hair neatly coiled in its usual arrangement on top of her head, she ran along the passage and tapped on her mother's door. She was immediately invited to enter.

'Come in, my dear, I have been waiting for you.' Her mother had also changed. 'What do you think? Do I look presentable?'

'We have selected an identical colour, Mama. Dressed as we are, I doubt that either of our guests will be able to distinguish between mother and daughter.'

Her mother's happiness faded. 'Oh dear! I have no wish to be considered anything other than your mama. I shall change at once into something more suitable.'

'No, please do not, you look lovely. It is hardly your fault that you have not aged as other women do. We shall go down together.

If the gentlemen are in the breakfast parlour before us then we had better not be tardy, or there will be nothing left for us.'

Downstairs it was unpleasantly gloomy; they did not light candles during the day, but it was so overcast outside, just this once, Annabel thought, they should forget economy. 'It is very quiet, Mama. Our guests are either still abed or outside. I am going to ask Fred to light some candles. It is too depressing creeping about in the dark.'

The sound of unfamiliar footsteps approaching from the kitchen warned her one of their guests was about to join them. She felt her mother stiffen; it would be difficult for her to meet strangers after living so long in solitude. She prayed it would not be the objectionable Colonel Sinclair. But it was *he* who strode in to meet them quite unaware he was being observed.

'Good morning, Colonel Sinclair. I should like to present my mother, Lady Sophia to you.' She had the satisfaction of seeing the gentleman miss his footing at her unexpected remark. Hiding her smile, she stepped down into the hall taking her mother with her. It was only as he bowed rather too deeply, that she realized she had not introduced herself last night. Why was he viewing her mama with such sympathy?

41

'I am delighted to meet you, my lady, and I thank you for your kind hospitality.'

'I believe that you have already met my daughter, Annabel Bentley, sir.' Her mother smiled at the colonel's confusion. 'You and the major are most welcome at Brandon Hall.'

She squeezed her mother's elbow to indicate that they should curtail the conversation. Now she saw this gentleman fully clothed she was even more aware of his formidable size; he was not a man to trifle with. His odd behaviour was making her nervous. What if he was of an unstable disposition? It did not bear thinking of.

'Good day, Colonel Sinclair. Please make yourself at home. My mother and I do not mix in company.' Increasing the pressure on her mother's arm she half dragged her down the passageway and into the relative safety of the breakfast-room.

'Annabel, whatever has got into you, child? The poor man was totally bemused by your behaviour.'

'Did you not see, Mama, the way he looked at you so strangely? I did not tell you exactly what transpired last night. I'm not sure the colonel is of sound mind. We had better not spend any time in his company after all.'

Her mother looked at her as if *she* was the

one deranged. 'You have wasted far too much time reading lurid novels, my love. If there is anything amiss with that gentleman, then I shall eat my best bonnet!'

★　★　★

Robert heard the unexpected voice coming from above him and almost fell over his feet. He looked round to see the young lady he had met en déshabillé last night clutching the arm of a woman who could be her sister, but he knew to be her unbalanced mother.

He noticed the girl was hanging on to the woman's arm; he wondered in what way the unfortunate lady's madness was manifested. If he smiled and treated her gently, perhaps she would remain calm. He bowed to Lady Sophia and was surprised to hear her welcome him with perfect clarity.

Before he could introduce himself correctly Miss Bentley dragged her mother away. He watched them vanish into the breakfast parlour and sighed. It was a sad day indeed to find a situation such as this. The family had obviously banished the unstable Lady Sophia to live in isolation where she could harm no one and cause no embarrassment. Her daughter had volunteered to take care of her mother.

It was a great shame that Miss Bentley's beauty must remain hidden, that a young girl should be obliged to give up her own life in this way. He knew nothing about insanity; he would discuss the matter with Dudley when eventually he came down to join him.

Maybe there was some way he could help them? He grinned. He had not felt so enthused since . . . his happiness faded. He did not deserve to feel anything but bleak — what had happened to Maria had been his fault.

4

The breakfast-table was laid with two places. It was plain that their guests had not eaten this morning either. 'Mama, I don't wish to sit at the table with two strange gentlemen. We have only their word, after all, that they are who they say they are.'

'What nonsense! They arrived in an expensive carriage drawn by four magnificent bays. Colonel Sinclair was immaculately attired. It might be some time since I moved in high society, but I recognize the cut of an expert in his jacket. He also has impeccable manners.'

'It is what is inside the jacket that counts. I do not like him and he shall not win me over with pretty smiles.' She walked briskly to the servant's exit. 'I shall go and fetch our breakfast, Mama, but I shall not remain in the room if our guests appear.'

On arrival in the kitchen she discovered both men comfortably seated at the enormous scrubbed table that ran down the centre of the room. Two heads turned as one and two overlarge gentlemen sprang to their feet and bowed. Before she could retreat, the colonel stepped forward.

'Miss Bentley, allow me to present Major Simon Dudley.'

She did no more than nod in acknowledgement then turned to speak to Mary who was frying ham and eggs in a skillet on the range. 'If our food is ready, Mary, I shall take it in. You are obviously busy here.' She supposed that the colonel would replace the ham and eggs as well as the brandy he had consumed last night!

'You gave me a right turn, standing there, miss,' Mary said, fanning her face with the cloth she had been holding a pan handle with.

It was only then that Annabel remembered as far as the staff were concerned she and her mother were still incarcerated in the attic. How could she have been so stupid! Her wits were wandering this morning, no doubt caused by lack of sleep.

'I am so sorry, Mary, Lady Sophia decided that as Colonel Sinclair had already discovered I was in residence we might as well come down again.' What the two listeners made of this she had no inkling; they were uninvited visitors and it mattered not to her what they thought.

'You shouldn't be out here, Miss Bentley. When my Fred's finished in the sick-room he'll bring your breakfast right along.'

She should have enquired after the health of the injured groom herself; she did not think of herself as an uncaring person, so why had she forgotten the very existence of this man? 'How is the patient doing? Do we need to send for a physician?' She had addressed all her remarks to Mary, keeping her back firmly turned on the two interested listeners. A slight movement and a cough behind her reminded her they were there. Reluctantly she spun round to face them.

'Billy has a slight concussion, nothing worse, he will be up and about in no time, Miss Bentley.'

'I'm so glad he's recovering, Colonel. Let us hope Fred and Thomas can as speedily repair your wheel. You will wish to continue your journey as soon as possible; no doubt you will be missed at Brandon Manor.'

There was a flash of what could have been anger in his eyes, but his expression remained open and amiable. 'I can assure you, Miss Bentley, we shall be on our way the moment my vehicle is roadworthy. We have no wish to be a burden on your limited resources, and we will take our meals in here and thus leave you and Lady Sophia in peace in the main part of the house.'

She nodded a second time and smiled

frostily. 'You are most accommodating, sir. Lady Sophia and I are unused to entertaining as you are obviously aware; however, do not feel obliged to eat in the kitchen, we shall leave the small sitting-room for your use whilst you are with us.'

Mary, unaware of the undercurrent of ill feeling that accompanied this conversation, chimed in cheerily, 'These gentlemen don't mind eating in here, miss; they are military men and are used to eating in far rougher places than this. But if your mind's set on them having the small parlour for their own then I shall get on to it as soon as breakfast is done.'

'Thank you, Mary. I shall leave you to continue your cooking. The fire is lit in the breakfast-room, I shall occupy myself with making toast until Fred is ready to serve us.'

She swept from the room almost colliding with Tom Hopkins who had just come in through a side door, and seemed unsurprised to see her. 'Good morning, Miss Bentley. It's right nasty out there, I can tell you. The river's flooded; I reckon the wheel will be ready long before the road is passable again.'

Her heart dipped to her boots at his bald statement. 'Oh no! I feared as much. It could be two weeks before the water subsides.' She had quite forgotten the kitchen door was still wide open and her conversation clearly heard by the occupants.

'Them gentlemen from London ain't going nowhere for a while, that's for sure.' The expression of comical dismay on Thomas's face when he finally registered that all the elaborate preparations, countless rehearsals, had been for naught, made her smile.

'I know; it was all a ridiculous waste of time. We were discovered so easily by our visitors. I am glad at least that it was strangers whom we attempted to deceive and not Sir Randolph.'

'Sir Randolph? Would that be Sir Randolph Rushton by any chance, Miss Bentley?'

All desire to laugh evaporated. How could she have been so stupid as to mention *his* name? She felt her stomach lurch and clutched at the wall for support. She wanted to deny she had spoken, but it was too late, the expression on the colonel's face told her after four years in hiding they were discovered. Before she could protest he had stepped forward and scooped her up into his arms.

'Miss Bentley is unwell. Direct me to a chamber in which she can recover her composure.'

She was aware that Major Dudley and Mary had appeared in the doorway, but was too embarrassed and humiliated to do more than hide her face in the shoulder of the man who had snatched her willy-nilly into his arms.

★ ★ ★

'Dudley, you are down at last. I have arranged for us to eat in the kitchen. Come into the small parlour we used last night and I shall explain my reasons to you.' As soon as they were private and the door firmly closed he explained. 'We are not alone here, a girl and her insane mother are living here. I met the young woman in the kitchen when I came down for a drink in the middle of the night.'

'God's teeth! Which of you was the more shocked by the encounter?'

'The honours were equal, my friend. I must warn you, she is the most beautiful creature I have ever set eyes on.'

'I hope you're telling me it's a *coup de foudre*. It's high time you moved on from what happened in Spain.'

'Stow it! I've done nothing of the kind. Miss Bentley is different — I could perhaps come to like her.' Before Dudley could interrupt he waved him into the seat waiting for him to settle before continuing, 'I met Lady Sophia, Miss Bentley's mother, just now. The two women are so alike they could be sisters. I doubt that Lady Sophia could have been more than a child herself when her daughter was born.'

'Indeed! I want to know what in God's name possessed the two of them to hide in the attics when we appeared?'

'I was coming to that; I was convinced that Lady Sophia is deranged. That would explain why the two of them are living here in isolation with so few staff. I believe it is not uncommon in society for an unfortunate to be locked away where they can cause no embarrassment to the family.'

'But now?' Major Dudley rubbed his chin. 'A conundrum indeed. It would certainly explain their strange behaviour. You said you met Lady Sophia this morning, did she seem insane in any way? Is that why you think it wiser for us to remain separate from them whilst we are here?'

'Actually, her ladyship appeared almost normal, if it hadn't been for the fact that her daughter was gripping her arm and was obliged to almost drag her away, I would have thought her completely *compos mentis*.'

'In which case, old fellow, I shall follow your lead in this matter. It is a great pity we are obliged to intrude on their privacy in this way, we must do everything we can not to disrupt the normal pattern of their lives. I seem to recall that sudden upsets and changes in routine can cause mania to become worse.'

The matter decided satisfactorily Robert changed the subject to that of the injured groom. 'I have already visited Billy and he is almost fully recovered. Apart from a lump on the back of his head he's as good as new. I told him to stay where he was today, and resume his duties tomorrow.'

'And your cattle? No doubt you have already checked on them as well.'

'I did that first; they have been well looked after, the stabling here is excellent. I think there must be horses somewhere else, or why would there be so many boxes ready for use?'

Major Dudley stood up. 'Now the secret is out, I expect the animals will reappear. I hope they came to no harm in the storm last night.'

'Tom, the housekeeper's husband, and the young man, Fred, I think he was called, were nowhere to be seen this morning. I expect they were taking care of the missing animals.'

Together they strolled back through the narrow passageways until they reached the kitchen. Robert pushed the door open and was pleased to find the housekeeper busy at the range. 'Good morning, Hopkins. With your permission, Major Dudley and myself would much prefer to eat in here. I'm sure that you understand my reasons for requesting this.'

The woman frowned for a moment and then beamed. 'Of course, sir, you don't want to make any more work for us than you have to. Perhaps you could eat your breakfast in the kitchen, but dine in the small sitting-room you used last night?'

'Thank you, that would be an excellent compromise. Is that ham I can smell?' He sniffed appreciatively. 'We shall not require anything different from the food you serve yourselves; and I can assure you that as soon as we are able to, your larder shall be refilled at our expense.'

His friend was already seated at the central table and he joined him there, knowing his presence was unsettling the housekeeper. Two steaming cups of tea were placed in front of them, quickly followed by a plate of freshly baked bread, butter and bramble jelly.

He was happily munching his second piece of bread and conserve when the door swung open and Miss Bentley came in. The look of astonishment on the housekeeper's face told him that the girl had not informed her staff that she and her mother were no longer hiding in the attics.

The young lady was decidedly terse, barely

acknowledging his introduction of his friend. If there was one thing that set his teeth on age, it was ill manners; *common courtesy costs nothing* was a famous saying of his. He caught Dudley's eye and shrugged and his friend smiled, seemingly unbothered by his dismissal.

Miss Bentley, her message delivered — that she and her mother would be eating in the breakfast parlour — walked out leaving the door ajar and he was able to overhear the conversation between the girl and Tom Hopkins.

He moved forward intending to close the door when Tom mentioned the road was flooded and that it would be impassable for a week or more. He had to know more of this and stepped out into the corridor; as he did so he heard her mention the name of someone he knew.

'Sir Randolph? Would that be Sir Randolph Rushton by any chance, Miss Bentley?'

At his comment the girl's head jerked up and her face drained of colour, her look of horror as she staggered against the wall told him he had by chance discovered a secret. Miss Bentley must be of a sickly disposition; she was certainly as slender as a wand and this was the second time he had seen her swoon.

Without conscious thought he was beside her and lifting her into his arms. Her collapse was his fault, it was up to him to put matters right. Ignoring her feeble protest he demanded that the open mouthed servant direct him immediately to a suitable room. He shouted back to the housekeeper. 'Hopkins, your young mistress is unwell, you must come at once to attend to her. Major Dudley can finish cooking the breakfast for you.'

★   ★   ★

Annabel knew wriggling would be useless, the colonel was a military man and used to getting his own way. It would be better if she kept still until he put her down in the drawing-room. She shuddered to think what her poor mama would think of the situation. She was not left long to wonder.

'Good heavens! Might I ask exactly what is going on here, Colonel Sinclair?' Her mother's voice ripped through the corridor. She recognized the danger signals, but the man, who was carrying her, did not.

He ignored the question and continued on his way to the front of the house. Should she warn him, or wait and see how he reacted to her mother in one of her furies? She had

55

learnt, when still in leading strings, to desist instantly when spoken to in *that* particular tone.

Something prompted her to pull sharply on his jacket collar. 'Colonel Sinclair, you must not ignore my mama. When she is angry it is best to take evasive action if you wish to remain intact.'

Instead of responding he nodded, his expression sympathetic. 'I understand, Miss Bentley, but I shall not be deterred. When I have found you somewhere comfortable to rest shall be time enough to deal with Lady Sophia.'

He shouldered his way into the drawing-room and deposited her gently on the *chaise-longue*. She thought it expedient to dissemble; she sighed loudly and settled back as if in a further fit of the vapours. With her eyes closed she prayed that her mother might be more concerned for her health than venting her spleen on the unfortunate colonel. At the sound of footsteps she clenched her fists and waited.

'Colonel Sinclair, I must assume that you have the double affliction of deafness and lack of intellect to burden you. Is Major Dudley your keeper? If so, he is doing a demonstrably poor job.'

He had, for some reason, remained

positioned beside her as if she needed protecting from her mother. From under her eyelashes she saw him stiffen, outraged at her mother's insults.

'Madam, it is not *my* faculties that are suspect. Miss Bentley was taken unwell and I was obliged to carry her somewhere she could be comfortable. However your muddled mind might like to view this, I can assure you my motives were of the most honourable.'

It was only then that she recalled her concern about his mental equilibrium. If she was not mistaken, he had just accused *Mama* of being insane. It was time for her to make a miraculous recovery.

'Oh dear! Whatever is all this shouting? How did I come to be in here? Mama, is that you?' The colonel's head shot around to stare at her as if it was *she* who had now become a candidate for Bedlam.

'My darling girl, you have never fainted in your life. I do hope you are not going down with the fever.' Her mother, ignoring the formidable gentleman glowering down at her, dropped to her knees.

'I am feeling decidedly peculiar, Mama. I should like to be alone.'

He took the hint and, with a fulminating stare, he strode off, his back parade-ground stiff. It was going to take a deal of explaining to smooth matters over. It did not bode well for the next two weeks if she could not arrange for her mother and the colonel to be civil to each other.

As if in punishment for feigning illness, her head had now begun to pound in earnest and she knew she was about to suffer from one of her fearsome megrims. The door opened and Mary hurried in.

'Whatever next! Here you are prostrate on the day-bed, miss, and the colonel has slammed out of the house and not touched his ham and eggs.'

5

Robert strode round to the stables not sure why he was so angry. Lady Sophia was deranged, so he could hardly blame her for being insubordinate. He would take one of the horses and see for himself just how bad the flooding was; it would give him time to calm down.

He tacked up, vaulting into the saddle as if about to lead a cavalry charge, and cantered out of the yard scattering fowl in all directions. It wasn't until he was halfway down the drive that he understood what had angered him. If Lady Sophia was in any way half-witted then so was he. In which case, why had they been hiding in the attic?

The sound of rushing water interrupted his musings. He reined back and stood in his stirrups, shocked to see what had once been a narrow lane was now a torrent of muddy water. Hopkins was right, no carriage would be able to pass this way for some considerable time. It was a damn good thing they hadn't written to announce their arrival at Brandon Manor; circumstances being as they were Dudley's sister would have been left wondering what had happened to them.

Feeling more relaxed he cantered parallel to the river until he was prevented from continuing by a large five-barred gate. From here he could watch the water rush by, it covered not just the lane but the field on the far side. It was only because Brandon Hall was set above the surrounding countryside that his mount was not up to his hocks in the flood.

Indeed, this new river had encroached into the lower levels of the parkland, but it would go no further. Even when the waters receded he doubted if the lane would be passable: it would be mud-filled and dangerously slippery; he had seen similar cases in Spain. It could be days before the waters subsided. He frowned as he considered the disagreeable option that faced him; he and Dudley could ride the ten miles across country and return to collect their carriage at the end of their visit, or they could remain *in situ*.

Lady Sophia had taken him in dislike, and he knew he was not favourably disposed towards her either. However, it was her daughter who presented the real problem. At eight and twenty he had been the youngest colonel in Wellington's army. At thirty he was considered an eligible *parti*. He was not as deep in the pocket as some of his cronies but was warm enough. He had inherited a neat estate in Hertfordshire which brought him in a tidy income, and his prize money, securely deposited in the funds, was increasing in value every year. An unattached hero from the Peninsular, with an annual income of £3,000, might be just what Miss Bentley was looking for. After what had happened to Maria he had vowed to remain celibate, but the way the young woman stirred his senses could prove disastrous. Being cloistered here for two weeks could leave them both compromised.

She was an innocent. Good God! Had she not already appeared inappropriately dressed and actually taken hold of his hand? Her mother was more worldly, had understood immediately that he had overstepped the bounds of propriety by holding her daughter in that intimate fashion. Had Miss Bentley now told her mother what had taken place in the kitchen the previous night? Would he return to find Lady Sophia insisting that he did the honourable thing? This could not happen. He must not weaken. What he felt for her was desire, nothing else. He would suggest to Dudley that they packed their bags and rode across country to Brandon Manor this afternoon. Billy and Jethro must remain behind and make themselves useful.

★   ★   ★

It was two wretched days before Annabel recovered from her sick headache. She opened her eyes to find sunlight streaming into the bedroom, her head clear and her stomach settled. Relieved that she was well, she scrambled out of bed and hurried into the dressing-room. There was sufficient cold water in the jug for her to wash. Twenty minutes later, her hair in a plaited coronet, dressed in her riding habit, she was on her way downstairs to find something to eat before going to the stables.

Mary was kneading dough at the table. 'Good morning, miss, you look a deal better today. There's no fresh bread yet, but I can soon do you some eggs, and the water is boiling ready for tea.'

'Is there stale bread? I can toast it in front of the range, I don't require anything cooked today, thank you, Mary.' She had expected to find the kitchen already occupied by their two guests.

'Have Colonel Sinclair and Major Dudley not come down yet?'

'Heavens! Did Lady Sophia not tell you? They left yesterday on horseback. They intend to collect their carriage and their men when they return from their visit.'

She was not sure if she was relieved or disappointed to find their visitors departed so suddenly. Still, she would meet them again when they came back. 'How long will it take Fred to repair the wheel axle, do you know?'

'He reckons it should be done by the end of the week, but it will be another week after that before the lane is suitable for vehicles.' Mary handed her three slices of bread and a toasting fork and placed a cup of tea on the table beside her. 'There you are, you'll feel all the better for eating something.'

She busied herself cooking her bread and when the first slice was done to her satisfaction she covered it thinly with butter, ignoring the bramble jelly. Her delicate digestion was not ready for sweet treats. 'Have the colonel's two retainers gone with him, Mary?'

'Bless you, miss, no. Billy is fully recovered and helping Fred repair the wheel. Jethro is working with my Tom in the vegetable garden. It's a real godsend, having those two here when there's so much to do to prepare for the winter.'

'I'm sorry you have to work so hard; I wish I could do more to help.'

'You mustn't fret, miss, we're happy enough, wouldn't want to be anywhere else.' She pushed an errant strand of grey-brown hair back under her cap and beamed. 'And a bit of hard work never hurt anyone, and you do quite enough. It ain't right for a lady to do so much. You should be sewing and such, not shovelling and digging like common folk have to.'

'I should go mad with boredom, Mary, and well you know it. I play the pianoforte, and help in the still room, they are ladylike pursuits, as I'm sure you will agree.' Brushing crumbs from her skirt she stood up. 'Could you tell Mama that I am going out when she comes down? Silver will be desperate for exercise; it's three days since he has been ridden.'

'It's grand to see you in a habit, miss, and not in britches and boots. Will your beast take a side saddle safely?'

'Good grief! I shall still ride astride, Mary. My only concession to propriety this morning was to don my habit; remember it has a divided skirt, it works well which ever saddle I use.'

Outside, the autumn sun turned the flagstones from grey to silver, but she ignored them, such poetical fancies were her mother's domain. One artist in the family with their head in the clouds, was sufficient. She liked to keep her feet firmly on the ground; without her practical skills she was certain they could not have survived on so little money for so long.

The stable yard was empty; her horse, a huge, dapple-grey gelding, was stamping impatiently in his box. She hurried across and called to him.

'Silver, here I am, sweetheart. I shall have your tack ready in an instant; you must be patient for a while longer.'

The massive head swung over the box to greet her. She pulled his ears and kissed him fondly on his velvet nose. 'Have you missed me, Silver? Good boy. Stand still whilst I fetch your saddle and bridle.' She was relieved to see the horse had been groomed and fed, all she had to do was get him ready. This was a task she always did herself, the animal was as gentle as a kitten with her, but ferocious with anyone else. Even Tom and Fred who had looked after him since he was a two year old still treated the gelding with caution.

She trotted out of the yard passing the barn in which the damaged axle was being repaired. She was surprised to find Fred hammering busily on his own. 'Where's Billy? I thought he was here helping you?'

The young man looked up from his task, getting hastily to his feet. 'He's ridden into Ipswich, miss. There's something I need to finish this task and he has errands to run for the colonel as well.'

'How ever will he find his way? He's a

stranger in Suffolk.'

'It ain't far across the fields, Miss Bentley, and he has a tongue in his head, don't he? I only need some particular nails; Billy will have no difficulty carrying those back.'

With this she had to be satisfied; she could not imagine what Colonel Sinclair had required of his groom to do in Ipswich. It was none of her concern. She would not worry about the young man's whereabouts, she would enjoy a gallop around the estate.

★   ★   ★

'There! I can see it; Brandon Manor — it can be no more than a mile ahead.'

'I shall be mightily glad to get there, Dudley, I have as much water in my boots as if I had been riding in a river.' Robert could see a handsome building of considerable size across the park. 'I hope that your sister does not stand on ceremony, we look like a pair of vagabonds descending on her.'

'Amelia will appreciate the effort we have made to get here. The fact that we are mud spattered and dishevelled will make no difference.'

Robert's mount was tiring after the arduous cross-country ride; the horse was more used to pulling his carriage than jumping fences and ditches in this way. 'Dudley, I should be loath to return the way we've come; I fear it has proved too much for these beasts. If they have not both suffered from tendon damage I shall be amazed.'

'Neither of them are lame. There are no further jumps to take, so we might as well walk the remaining distance, give them time to cool down.'

Two grooms greeted them in the stable yard on their arrival. Dudley dismounted and tossed his reins at the first. 'I am Major Dudley come to visit Lady Barton; this is Colonel Sinclair. Take special care of the horses, they are not used to what they have endured this morning.'

Robert glanced round the yard and found it satisfactory. He shook out the worst of the mud from his riding coat, then held out his hand for his carpetbag which had been tied precariously to the back of his saddle.

'I hope we are not expected to dress for dinner, neither of us has our evening rig.'

'I told you, Sinclair, my sister will be so delighted we are here at all she will take us as she finds us and make no complaints.'

★   ★   ★

This proved to be the case. Lady Barton was ecstatic to see them and could not hear enough about their adventures. Robert was pleased with his accommodation and had even been provided with a valet to take care of his every need. The man told him he had been Sir George's manservant and was grateful to have two gentlemen to take care of.

Amelia Barton was short and plump with nut-brown ringlets and a ready smile. The two small children were paraded briefly, but he had been hard put to tell whether they were male or female, both being dressed in frilly garments. He had had little to do with infants and, as he did not intend to marry, things would remain that way.

It had been fortuitous Miss Bentley had been obliged to stay in her rooms, as this had meant Lady Sophia had also been absent. When he had suggested to Dudley that they leave immediately for Brandon Manor his friend had been strangely reluctant. It had taken a deal of persuasion, but he had got his way. He always did.

Spruced up, with his boots shining, fresh britches and shirt and newly pressed jacket, he was ready to go down for dinner. Lady Barton kept country hours, for which he was heartily grateful. They had been riding since early morning and breakfast had been many hours ago, it was now four o'clock and he was more than ready to eat.

They were halfway through their meal when he recalled that the mention of Sir Randolph Rushton had caused Miss Bentley to recoil in horror. Perhaps he could find out more from his hostess. 'Lady Barton, have you heard of a family called Rushton? Sir Randolph Rushton, and Lady Sophia, to be exact.'

'Good heavens! I have not heard that name mentioned for several years now; it was a huge scandal, you know. Lady Sophia Rushton ran away, taking her daughter from her first marriage with her. It was the talk of the town at the time.'

Robert felt a shiver of apprehension. That was why the name was so familiar. Could it be the same man a fellow officer had told him about? He had not connected the two names until now. Sir Randolph Rushton was infamous for his debased practices and was a member of the Hellfire Club. No unprotected young woman was safe when he was near. The officer, Latimer, if he recalled correctly, had been obliged to rescue his own sister from the man's clutches. This had been no more than two or three years ago.

'Did Rushton make any effort to find his wife?' He stared hard at his friend warning him not to mention that they had met Lady Sophia and her daughter.

'Let me think. Yes, I believe he invested a deal of money in the search. He was heartbroken, you know, it was quite pitiful to see his misery. I cannot understand why his wife should wish to run away from such a charming and wealthy man.'

'Perhaps there was another gentleman involved? Whatever the reason, it is none of our business,' Dudley said firmly. His sister immediately changed the subject, obviously well used to following the instructions of her older brother.

When Lady Barton withdrew, leaving them to their port, Robert spoke urgently to his friend. 'Your sister is going to ask why I mentioned the man's name in the first place — what do you propose to tell her when she does? Do you know what the man is like?'

'I heard rumours. When his name was mentioned by Miss Bentley I knew instantly why they were hiding at Brandon Hall. Lady Sophia and her daughter must not be betrayed by us, their secret must be kept.'

'God's teeth!' Robert hurtled to his feet, his chair crashing noisily to the floor behind him. 'I told Billy to go into Ipswich to replace the brandy we drank. What if he overheard Miss Bentley? The boy's room opened on to the corridor. My God! He could unwittingly betray them and that bastard could turn up

70

and drag them off. It would be my fault.'

He heard his chair being replaced and then his friend gripped him by the shoulder. 'Do not overreact in this way, Sinclair. Even if Billy mentions Lady Sophia or Miss Bentley whilst in Ipswich, why should anyone report the matter to a London aristocrat?'

'Ipswich is not so very far from Town; a careless word spoken today could reach London by tomorrow.' He felt his pulse slowing as he recovered from his agitation. 'That man was trying to ensnare unwary young ladies a little over two years ago. Perhaps he has moved on and forgotten about his missing wife and step-daughter.'

Surely it could not be happening a second time? He sank back on his chair, pouring himself another glass of port to steady his nerves. He had a bad feeling about this; his military instincts were aroused. Rushton might well not give up until he had reclaimed what he would consider to be his property. Lady Sophia must have run away to protect her daughter. She would have been the same age as Latimer's sister.

'Let's hope so, Sinclair. We don't need to worry about Lady Sophia and her daughter at the moment. Remember, the road is impassable and likely to remain that way for a sennight at least.'

'Of course, you're correct — my wits are wandering. We shall be returning there shortly and can see for ourselves that they are safe.'

Was this his opportunity to redeem himself? In protecting these two women from Rushton would he finally be able to put the past behind him?

★   ★   ★

Several days passed pleasantly enough at Brandon Manor, but Robert's thoughts constantly turned to the occupants of Brandon Hall. He wished he had not departed so precipitously, but had stayed to get to know Miss Bentley's circumstances better.

There had been no further rain and according to the head gardener the floods everywhere were receding and the roads would be usable soon. He would risk his carriage horse a second time and ride back to Brandon Hall the following day. Dudley did not wish to remain behind. Although he had not seen his sister or her children for several years, he was adamant he would leave the next day.

Robert was in the stable yard discussing the advisability of bandaging the legs of both horses before they attempted the return journey when he heard galloping hoofs and a huge grey gelding thundered through the archway its rider bringing his mount to a rearing halt.

6

Lady Sophia was waiting in the drawing-room to greet Annabel when she came down after changing out of her riding habit. 'My dear, are you feeling better? Did you gallop out the last of your headache?'

'I did, thank you, Mama. I was most surprised to find our visitors gone. I do hope you and the colonel were able to be civil to each other before they left.'

'Ah! The colonel, I must talk to you about that gentleman. Come and sit down, I asked Mary to bring a tray here as soon as you returned.'

Annabel knew this was a gentle warning not to mention Colonel Sinclair until after their lunch had been delivered to them. She hurried to open the door at the rattle of crockery approaching. 'Here, Mary, let me take that from you. You have more than enough to do with two extra mouths to feed.'

'Thank you, miss, but you leave it here and I will send my Fred along to collect it later. I reckon that Billy won't be back until this evening, so only one extra for this meal.'

Chuckling to herself the housekeeper vanished back into the bowels of the house.

The tray contained vegetable broth, sweet rolls and apple pie; more than enough for a luncheon. Annabel arranged the food on the table whilst her mother drew up two chairs.

'Sit down, my dear. Now, I want to know exactly what happened that night that you went down and met Colonel Sinclair in the kitchen.'

Annabel had been dreading this moment and her cheeks flushed painfully. By the time she had explained the whole she knew it was far worse than she had thought.

'Good grief! He in his shirt and britches only? And you took his hand in yours?' Her mother shook her head in disbelief.

'He had burnt himself, Mama, I was helping him — '

'It is all my fault,' her mother interrupted, her voice little more than a whisper. 'I have failed in my duty as a parent. If I had explained to you how to go on then this would never have happened. I am so sorry, my darling, I have ruined your life along with my own.'

She was well used to her mother being over dramatic but this was more extreme than usual. 'Mama, you have nothing to apologize for. Colonel Sinclair is a gentleman, what took place between us will never be mentioned elsewhere. I fully understand that I compromised myself by remaining in the kitchen, unchaperoned, as I did. However, no damage has been done as far as I can see. My reputation remains intact.' She grinned at her mother, hoping to lighten the mood. 'But I'm eager to hear what you did whilst I was unwell that could possibly have ruined *your* reputation.'

'It is nothing to jest about, Annabel. I ruined my life when I married that monster: a runaway wife is permanently beyond the pale.'

Instantly contrite, Annabel reached out and clasped her mother's hands. 'I beg your pardon, Mama. Please, let's forget about our unexpected visitors and try and get on with our lives in the quiet way we have done for these past years.' She picked up her spoon and tasted the soup. 'Come, you must eat. This is delicious — by far the best carrot and spinach broth that Mary has made this year. Remember, Mama, what you are always saying to me about making the most of God's bounty when we have it?'

'You are right to remind me, my love. I shall not repine; what is done is done, we shall look to the future together. However, meeting the two gentlemen from London has made me realize how much you're missing living here with me.'

'I am perfectly happy, I have no interest in new gowns and suchlike. Now, Mama, tell me, did you make your peace before they left?'

'Unfortunately I had no opportunity to do so. However, I did have a most enjoyable conversation with Major Dudley. I was occupied with you for the remainder of the day and the following morning they had gone by the time I came down.' She smiled. 'Major Dudley did leave me a letter thanking me for my hospitality and promising to return to collect the carriage and the remainder of the team in two weeks' time. He also left ten guineas to cover the costs involved.'

'Mama! That's a fortune. It will pay for our winter fuel and leave sufficient over to purchase a few extras for the festive season.'

Later she retreated to the music room and her beloved pianoforte. Soon the house was filled with music and she was able to forget the irascible Colonel Sinclair and his friend. When she eventually closed the instrument it was to discover she had an audience of one.

'That was magical, my darling. I could sit and listen to you play all day. Look, I have not been idle sitting here.' Lady Sophia held up a sketch for her approval.

'Good heavens! I look quite demented — are you quite sure you have got my expression correct?'

Arm in arm they returned to the breakfast parlour where dinner was to be served. The food was fresh from the garden, and although plain it was cooked to perfection.

'Mary has excelled herself with this roast capon, Mama. I wonder which one of the cockerels we are eating tonight.'

'Annabel! What a horrid thing to say; you have quite put me off my dinner.' Her mother put down her cutlery with a sigh. 'Billy has not returned. Jethro is quite concerned about the young man; he fears he has been taken poorly, that his concussion was more serious than we thought.'

'I'm sure nothing untoward has occurred. He has the wherewithal to stay overnight, so that is probably what he has done. It is a long ride to Ipswich, he could well have felt too fatigued to attempt the return journey today.'

'Let us hope so. I'm going to retire early tonight, my love. I wish to get up at dawn and paint the flood waters before they disappear. I have done it several times before, but never when the leaves are turning golden and russet, as they are now.'

'I shall do the same; I must get into the

orchard and pick the apples and what brambles there are left after the storm.'

★ ★ ★

The next morning Annabel dressed in her work clothes of men's britches, a thick flannel shirt, waistcoat, jacket and cap. The outfit was completed by sturdy boots, the sort that farm boys wore. With her hair tightly coiled and her cap pulled down low, she doubted if she would be recognized; not that there was anyone in the vicinity to see her whether she was dressed in a ball gown or as she was this morning.

She spent all day harvesting and by dusk had several baskets full of apples. The unblemished fruit would be stored in the root cellar under the kitchen. With luck there would be enough to see them through the winter. Tired and filthy she trudged inside coming face to face with Billy as she passed the barn.

'When did you return? I hope you are quite well after your trek into Ipswich?'

The young man doffed his cap and grinned. 'I got back around noon, Miss Bentley. I made so many purchases I did not dare risk travelling through the fields in the dark. There were rumours in Ipswich that there are troublemakers, rick burners, and soldiers returned from the wars with no work to do. I could have been waylaid and robbed, and the colonel would have been angry.'

'Well, I'm glad that you have returned safely. When will the carriage be repaired do you think?'

'Fred says the day after tomorrow, and the water's going from the lane. If it stays dry, Tom reckons it will be passable next week.'

She wondered why Sinclair should be angry if his groom was robbed? Surely he would be concerned for Billy's safety? She increased her pace, her fatigue forgotten in her eagerness to see what purchases had been made.

Scraping her boots outside the door, she stepped into the corridor and leant against the wall in order to remove them. She was about to head directly to the kitchen, when she heard her mother calling her.

Pausing at the bottom of the stairs she replied, 'Mama, I'm going upstairs to change out of my work clothes. I'm certain you do not wish me to appear dressed as I am.'

'Nonsense! I cannot wait that long, I want you to see what the Colonel and Major Dudley have sent us.'

Such excitement was seldom seen at Brandon Hall. She couldn't remember the last time she had seen her mother so exhilarated. She hurried along the passageway to join Lady Sophia who was waiting in the small parlour.

'At last! I have been beside myself with impatience since Billy returned. I could not possibly open the parcels on my own.'

Spread out on to side tables were a variety of interestingly shaped packages. No wonder the poor boy had not been able to set out in the dark without fear of being attacked by footpads.

'You did not have to wait for me, Mama, but I am very glad that you have.' She pointed at two bottle-shaped parcels. 'Those must be brandy. Colonel Sinclair promised he would replace those, did he not?'

'He did indeed; he also promised to replenish the larder, but I must admit to having examined all the gifts and I can smell nothing that reminds me of the kitchen.' Her mother rushed across the room and snatching up one of the brown paper-covered objects tossed it towards Annabel. Only by leaping forward did she manage to catch the parcel before it crashed to the floor.

Hugging it to her chest she stared at her mother in astonishment. 'Mama, what has got into you? If I dropped this it would have been such a waste.'

81

'Open it, my love. Do not stand there procrastinating, I wish to know immediately what is in that package. Remember I have already examined all of them — that one is soft, it could not possibly have broken even if you dropped it. When you have opened yours then I shall have my turn.'

The string was easily undone and brown paper quickly followed and a riot of brightly coloured material filled her hands. She held up the contents. 'It is a cashmere wrap; the colour is so vibrant I am sure it is intended for you.'

'Oh dear! It is rather bright; I am not surprised it is not quite what one would have wished, but one could hardly expect a groom to have knowledge of what might be pleasing to us.'

'Never mind, the colonel is trying to make amends. I doubt if he has much knowledge of feminine requirements; after all a man who travels without a manservant and with only one change of garments is hardly likely to understand the niceties of fashion.'

'That's as might be, my dear; his clothes were plain, but they were made by the best. The cut and material were excellent.'

Like children they tore off the paper in turn, exclaiming and gasping as each gift was revealed. There were paint-brushes, paper and charcoal and several folios of music, plus a variety of knickknacks and gee-gaws. When the last gift was revealed the floor was strewn with paper and string.

'Well! How could that gentleman possibly have known I was an artist? Or that you played the pianoforte for pleasure?'

'He must have gone into your studio, Mama, and also discovered how well thumbed my current music is. It was incredibly thoughtful of him. His instructions to Billy must have been so precise, I cannot imagine the boy would have thought of this for himself.' She scrambled to her feet. 'I shall go at once and ask him.'

'Do not forget to thank him as well, my dear.'

Mary was putting the fruit glaze upon a plum cake. 'Did you open all the parcels, miss? There was a fine ham, a box of marchpane and chocolate for your morning drink. I knew as soon as I saw those gentlemen that they were generous folk.'

'I cannot imagine how Billy was able to transport so much on the back of one horse. I am going to thank him for his effort.'

'He's in the barn with Fred, but you don't have to, miss, he was only doing his duty.'

Annabel knew it wasn't necessary to thank him in person, but there was something she particularly wished to ask him. He was busy hammering and looked up as she came in.

'Billy, Lady Sophia and I wish to thank you for bringing back so much from Ipswich. However, could you tell me how you selected the objects?'

He grinned. 'It weren't me, Miss Bentley. I just took this note into the emporium. I reckon as the colonel left it up to them to select the items.'

'That would explain it; is this why your errand took so long?'

He nodded vigorously. 'By the time I got there, it was after midday, and the shopkeeper reckoned it weren't long enough for him to make up the list. Everything had to be packed so's I could get it on the horse, they found me two panniers, which worked a treat.'

Her lips twitched; this would explain the eclectic mix of items they had received. The colonel must just have given instructions for things suitable for two ladies to be included without specifying the age of either. 'Did you go especially to buy music and artist's materials?'

'No, Miss Bentley, they must have been on the list as well.'

'I shall not hold you up any longer, Billy. Thank you again, Lady Sophia and I are delighted with the items.'

Delighted was perhaps too strong a word; surprised and amused would better describe how they had felt on discovering two satin pincushions, a silver inkwell, half-a-dozen handkerchiefs with lace edging, two books of boring sermons, and a miscellany of items to place on their dressing-tables.

It was, as Mama would no doubt say, the thought that counted. And certainly no expense had been spared. What they had received was far more than they had given in hospitality, and the money more than covered the expense of keeping two horses and mending the carriage.

★   ★   ★

Two days after receiving the unexpected gifts Annabel was working in the orchard when she heard a commotion in the stable yard. She was about to jump down from her perch in a particularly tall apple tree when the noise turned to shouts and a sudden scream of agony. She froze, too terrified to move.

What was happening? Were they being attacked by the renegades Tom had spoken of? Then she saw at least five roughly dressed men emerge from the yard and head towards the house. She was hidden from view where she was. There was nothing she could do. If she protested she would be captured, or worse. That would help no one.

The sound of shouting in the distance jolted her into action. She half fell from the tree and, keeping low, raced round to the stable yard, pausing to peer round the archway before bursting in. Her knees buckled at the carnage she saw there. Four bodies lay spread eagled on the cobbles. Forgetting the danger to herself she ran forward praying that these were not cadavers, that the men had not been murdered by the intruders.

She dropped to her knees by Tom who groaned. There was a hideous gash on the back of his head, but at least he was still alive. She moved quickly to Fred. He, too, was unconscious from a blow, but breathing evenly. Moving silently she reached Jethro. He was stretched out on his back. It was too late: his eyes were glazed, his jaw slack, his head at a peculiar angle.

She turned away to cast up her accounts, too shocked to care if anyone overheard her distress. Wiping her mouth on her sleeve she straightened and stared at Billy; he was leaning against the wall, his hands clutched to his side. She could see a red stain on his jacket, blood seeping through his fingers.

For a moment she was paralyzed, shock

rendering her incapable of rational thought. The men could be back at any moment, having ransacked the house they might return to take the horses and complete their grisly task by finishing off the three injured men.

A groan from Billy alerted her and she rushed to his side. The poor boy opened his eyes at her touch. 'You must get help, miss, ride to Brandon Manor and fetch the colonel and the major. They thought I had kicked the bucket; I heard them say they intended to hole up here for a few days.' He gasped, unable to speak for a moment. 'They must have followed me, or overheard me talking in the snug, it's all my fault.'

'Jethro is dead, but I believe Tom and Fred are merely unconscious. How badly have you been injured?'

'A knife in the side. I reckon I'll be all right in a moment. You get off, take your grey, don't worry about us, get help back here before they find Lady Sophia.'

'I shall take the other horses down to the meadow first, that will delay them if they do decide to leave.'

Billy didn't answer, he had swooned away. It was up to her now, but she didn't know what to do for the best. If she left for Brandon Manor would these men survive? She must pray that her mother and Mary were safe in the attic out of harm's way. She would try and help before she left. It was too late for Jethro. She steeled herself and walked across and pulled his eyelids down, then arranged his limbs in a more seemly manner.

What should she do? How could she prevent the murderers from completing their job? She looked around knowing she was not strong enough to move any of them, and if she fetched blankets then they would know someone else had been there.

A sound behind her spun her round. Billy was on his feet, a lopsided smile on his ashen face. 'I can take care of things here, Miss Bentley. You get your horse saddled and ride for help. Leave the other horses to me.'

Five minutes later she was astride Silver and galloping across the park. She had no definite direction to follow, but knew, for she had heard Jethro talk of it, that it was due east and as the crow flies, no more than eight miles. If she kept the sun behind her and looked out for a twisted church spire she would find her way.

Her horse devoured the miles, clearing enormous hedges and ditches without hesitation, and in less than an hour she saw the church spire and knew she was almost there. She urged her horse on, and they jumped a five-barred gate and she could see Brandon

Manor across the field.

'Come on, Silver, we're almost there. They are depending on us, we cannot fail them now.'

Her horse increased his pace; she knew he could gallop twice the distance without faltering. She guided him towards the rear of the building. She would be more likely to find assistance in the stables than at the front door. Despite the urgency, she was well aware that, dressed as she was, she was unlikely to gain entrance to such a grand establishment at the front of the house. Colonel Sinclair was standing in the yard talking to a groom. Thank God! She reined back violently. Her horse sat on his hocks, half rearing to a halt.

'Colonel Sinclair, you must come at once. Brandon Hall has been attacked and Jethro murdered.'

7

'God's teeth! Miss Bentley! I did not recognize you.' Robert surged forward and almost snatched the girl from the saddle. He expected her to fall tearfully into his arms and was taken aback by her resilience. She stepped away from him and repeated what she had shouted on her arrival.

'Colonel Sinclair, did you hear what I said? A band of renegades has taken over Brandon Hall, my mother is in extreme danger. You and the major must come at once to save her.'

He had not taken in the sense of her words the first time, had been too surprised by her sudden appearance dressed as a boy and riding a huge hunter better suited to a man. 'Jethro dead? What about the others?'

'Billy has been stabbed, but he is on his feet and says he can take care of Fred and Tom who have head injuries. I heard no sound of screaming when the men stormed the house so my mother and Mary must have managed to hide in the attics.'

'You there; get this horse rubbed down and walk him until he's cool. Then have your two best animals saddled. Major Dudley and I will be leaving as soon as I can find him.' He looked down at the mud-streaked young woman who had just ridden pell-mell over rough countryside and seemed hardly out of breath. She was a remarkable girl, he could have done with several troopers of her calibre when he was at Waterloo.

'Miss Bentley, you must come with me to the house. Lady Barton shall take care of you. Leave matters to us. I promise you Lady Sophia and your housekeeper shall be saved from harm.'

To his astonishment she shook her head, dislodging her cap and causing two stable boys, on the far side of the yard, to trip over their buckets in surprise. 'I shall do no such thing, sir, I am returning with you. Silver will be sufficiently rested by the time you are ready to leave. You will have noticed, I'm sure, that his breath is not laboured in the slightest.'

This would not do. He had given an instruction and he expected it to be followed to the letter. He drew himself to his full height and glared at her. 'That was not an invitation, young lady, it was an order. Either you accompany me on your own two feet or I shall sling you over my shoulder and carry you like a sack of potatoes. Which would you prefer?'

He saw a flicker of fear and expected her immediate capitulation, instead she dodged sideways to stand in front of her horse. Her expression of fury exactly matched his own. So be it. He was not going to be defied by little more than a schoolgirl. Good God, men twice her size had cowered beneath his anger.

'I should stop where you are, Colonel Sinclair. Silver is bigger than you. You cannot bully *him* into submission.'

★　★　★

Annabel saw his eyes darken and realized that this time she could have gone too far. Even her horse might not be sufficient to protect her. She pressed herself against his shoulder, one hand reaching up to entangle itself in his mane. The colonel had taken just two strides when Silver threw up his head and screamed defiance.

Too late to shout a warning; her horse was fiercely protective of her and didn't need to be told who was the enemy. The gelding would know the man with clenched fists approaching fast was his target. She spun round and threw both arms around the enraged beast's neck. 'Silver, you must not. I am in no danger, look he is our friend.'

Her horse ignored her words and plunged

forward, his head snaking out, ears flat to his skull, huge yellow teeth bared. The shout of pain as they sank into the colonel's shoulder gave her the strength to intervene. Spinning round she gripped the animal's lower lip twisting it viciously, forcing the beast to relinquish his hold.

Into the resulting chaos Major Dudley appeared at the double, word had obviously been sent to the manor of her arrival. She was swinging from the horse's mouth, the colonel white-faced, was rubbing his shoulder and the two grooms designated to tack up the most powerful hunters in the stable yard, were dithering about ineffectually not daring to intervene and get bitten or kicked by the flashing hoofs.

Suddenly two strong arms gripped her around the waist. 'Dudley take hold of the animal's bit. I shall remove Miss Bentley.'

She expected to be shouted at, after all her horse had just taken a lump out of the man she had come to ask for help. What had she been thinking of? If, instead of losing her temper, she had explained to him that she couldn't possibly go into the house dressed as she was without causing a scandal, none of this would have happened.

Her feet were slammed back to the cobbles, the force sending shockwaves up her legs. She shivered. He was still furious with her. 'Are you badly hurt, sir? I'm sorry, it was all my fault.' She didn't dare to raise her head to look at him.

'It certainly was. You could have been killed. If you had lost your grip you would have been trampled underfoot.' His tone was even, his words spoken softly, but she knew his anger was barely contained.

She had intended to agree with him, to beg his pardon, ask him to make haste as every minute counted. But when she opened her mouth something quite different emerged. 'My horse would never tread on me. It is *you* he would have trampled.'

'Is that before or after he tore me limb from limb?'

This unlikely remark sounded almost like a jest. Surely not? Her head shot up to meet not anger but amusement reflected on his face.

'You are an original; I must beg your pardon for ordering you as if you were a member of my regiment. Now, Miss Bentley, could you kindly explain to me why you were prepared to have me killed by your animal rather than go inside?'

'Good God!' Major Dudley interrupted. 'You didn't suggest she go inside dressed as she was? My sister would have had a fit of the vapours. Miss Bentley is far better out here with us.'

The look of incredulity on the colonel's face made her giggle. But the laughter became uncontrolled and soon she was sobbing wildly.

'My dear girl, this has been too much for you.'

She was grateful to be held against his chest until she shuddered to a stop. A large white handkerchief was stuffed into her hand. She blew her nose and mopped her cheeks.

He pushed her hair out of her eyes with a gentle hand. 'Are you feeling better? Here, drink this, it will restore you.' The metal of a flask top was pressed to her lips and she swallowed obediently. The fiery liquid surged through her body and she gasped.

'Thank you . . . I think. I should like a drink of water, and so would Silver now that he is cool.'

'Sit here, on this upturned tub, whilst I fetch you some. Major Dudley has gone back to inform Lady Barton what has happened. A footman has been sent to fetch the militia from Ipswich. I must leave you for a few minutes to collect what weaponry we can find in the gun-room.' He stepped away, concern on his face. 'I realize now that you must return with us, and you must have noticed I'm not familiar with propriety and etiquette.

To my mind it was more important that you had a hot bath and something to eat, rather than pander to Lady Barton's sensibilities.'

'I understand. Please don't worry about me, I'm used to taking care of myself. I'm more concerned with my mother's safety than my own fatigue. Could you hurry? We have already wasted far too long.'

He raised a hand as if he was going to touch her face again, and then dropped it, his lips curving into a slight smile. 'We shall be with you very soon. Take the time to catch your breath, it will be a hard ride back again.'

She watched him disappear at a run, relieved that Silver had not done him any permanent damage. He could not move so fast, or as easily, if his shoulder had been badly damaged. Closing her eyes, her head resting against the wall, she listened to the sounds of the stable yard. Its normality began to soothe her nerves and after a few minutes' respite she was ready to leave.

Where *was* Silver? She needed to check his feet for stones and re-saddle him so that he was ready when the men returned. The sound of a groom cursing in a box at the end of the row told her where her mount was. He would not let anyone, apart from her, deal with him.

'Let me do that. He does not like being handled and you will get bitten and stamped on for your trouble.'

The man slid past the flashing teeth with alacrity. 'If you're sure, miss, I'll leave you to it. He won't let me near him.'

By the time she heard pounding feet outside Silver was comfortable, his hoofs free of stones, his girth tightened and as eager to leave as she was. She led him out to find Colonel Sinclair bristling with weaponry. Both he and Major Dudley were wearing cavalry swords at their waists, and had pistols poking out of each pocket.

She looked for a mounting block, but the colonel stepped forward and tossed her into the saddle, his smile telling her he was confident of success. Gathering her reins she waited for her two escorts to be mounted, hoping that Brandon Manor had horseflesh up to their weight. As soon as the two geldings were led out she knew she had nothing to worry about. Whoever owned these magnificent animals must be a bruising rider, for both were well over sixteen hands and powerfully put together.

'Right; you lead the way, Miss Bentley. When we came we took the easiest route, neither of the animals we rode were up to our weight so we avoided the difficult terrain. We opened gates where we could, rather than jumping them.'

'We have to keep the sun in front, and ride due west. It took me less than an hour to get here, I hope we can return more quickly.'

She was about to move off when he rode up beside her. 'When we get within sight of your home we shall stop. It would do no good to announce our arrival. Leave things to us, surprise is on our side and have no fear, we shall prevail. We have faced more formidable opponents and come out unscathed many times.'

'My mother — '

'Lady Sophia will be unharmed, I give you my word.'

'Thank you, Colonel. I have the utmost confidence in both of you. Billy has told us you are both heroes of Waterloo; a handful of vagabonds should be as nothing to you.'

★　★　★

Robert had decided to send the girl ahead, not because he and Dudley could not find the quickest route themselves, but he wished her to set the pace. Her horse was strong, but galloping back might prove too much for it and he had no intention of leaving her unescorted in the wilds of Suffolk.

He had discussed with Dudley the best plan of action for when they arrived at

Brandon Hall. They would reconnoitre and, if there was no immediate danger to the ladies, they would wait until dark before attacking. He had promised that Lady Sophia would emerge unscathed from her ordeal, he could not say the same for the bastards who had killed his coachman and injured young Billy and the other two.

The two of them were hard pressed to keep up with the grey gelding and its diminutive rider. The girl flinched at nothing, setting her horse at the largest obstacles and sailing over with feet to clear. It was the Brandon Manor horses that were labouring by the time they were in sight of their destination.

'Miss Bentley, we are going to complete the rest of the journey on foot. You must remain here with the horses. Can you manage all three?' He had decided the best way to get the girl on side was to give her a challenge. As long as she was a safe distance from the house he cared little what she did. Taking care of three exhausted horses should fully occupy her time.

'I can, Colonel. If you hand me their reins, I shall walk them around until they are cooled down. I can take them to the meadow where we hid Silver last week. There is shelter, fodder and water there.' She knew exactly why he was so insistent she stayed with the

99

horses — he did not wish her to be underfoot when he ambushed the house. 'I am not stupid, Colonel Sinclair, I shall stay out of your way until the matter is dealt with.'

'Good girl. Is there somewhere you can curl up in the warm as well? It is quite possible we will not attack until full dark.'

'What about Tom and Fred? Can I not creep back to the stables and see if there's anything I can do to help them?'

An iron grip encircled her knee and she flinched. 'Absolutely not. I shall take care of them. You will remain out of harm's way, is that quite clear?'

This time she did not argue. 'I give you my word.'

The hand relaxed and he smiled, and for some strange reason her pulse skipped a beat. It must be anxiety that was playing havoc with it.

It was dusk, and from her vantage point on the back of a horse she could see the faint glimmer of candles in the hall. The intruders were obviously making themselves at home; she hoped they had found the brandy and drunk it all. Even two bottles between five or six men should blunt their senses enough to make it easier for the colonel and the major to accomplish their mission safely. They were brave men — Mama had been right to say

100

Providence had sent them.

It was odd how the major deferred to the colonel when he was his senior by several years. A wave of unexpected heat coloured her cheeks. Sinclair was autocratic and not at all the sort of man she could admire, so why did her heart flip when he so much as looked at her?

The three horses were exhausted and she had no difficulty walking them about the field until they were ready to be taken to the meadow. She gave the stables a wide berth; she had promised not to go there and would not break her word. It was difficult leading a horse on either side of her down the narrow track so she released the reins of one of the hunters and hoped it would follow its stable-mate.

There was just light enough to see to open the gate and take the horses through. She swung her leg over and dropped to the ground, her legs giving way beneath her. Silver's huge head nudged her in the back. 'I know, sweetheart, but I am as tired as you. Give me a moment and I shall be up again and take you somewhere warm and dry.'

Bracing herself against her horse she staggered to her feet. The three animals were waiting patiently to be tended to. Quickly removing their tack she hung it over the gate,

101

it would come to no harm there for the moment.

'You know the way, Silver, take the others down to the stream for a drink whilst I sort out your supper.' As if understanding her command the grey moved off towards the bottom of the field and the other two followed. She knew it was the scent of water that drew them, not her instructions.

The open barn had straw and hay piled at one end. All she had to do was find a pitchfork to shake out the bedding. It was dark inside the shelter and she had to do her work by touch. Fortunately, by the time the animals returned to investigate she had three mounds of sweet hay waiting and a thick layer of straw across the mud floor. Satisfied she had done all she could to make her charges comfortable she found herself a corner, out of harm's way, and settled down to wait.

Her stomach gurgled loudly. She hadn't eaten since dawn. She was also thirsty. Should she risk drinking from the brook that ran across the bottom of the field? No, not after the horses had been trampling in it. There were still apples on some of the trees in the orchard, that was nowhere near the stable yard or the house, so she wouldn't be breaking her promise by going there to find herself something to eat.

* ⋆ ⋆ ⋆

Robert wrapped his muffler around his head leaving only his eyes showing, then removed his cravat and buttoned up his jacket. He could hear his friend doing the same; they were well used to preparing for night-time raids. It was imperative to cover one's face and remove, or obscure, any light-coloured clothing. Too many men had foundered because they had forgotten this simple rule.

'There are candles lit in the house, I think we are safe to assume these bastards don't intend to leave tonight.'

'In which case, Sinclair, let's see how things are with the men. I brought my medical kit with me.'

Holding his scabbard in order to stop the sword rattling, Robert arrived at the stable block, Dudley close behind. He had excellent night vision and could see at a glance that apart from the corpse there were no other figures on the cobbles. He moved stealthily through the yard and out to the barn. He was sure that was where he would find the injured men.

'Billy? Billy, are you in there?' He tapped three times on the wall and was rewarded by movement inside. 'We're coming in, lad, stay put and wait for us.' Fingering his way along the wooden surface he came to the latch and quietly lifted it. He could see nothing; it was black as pitch inside.

'Over here, sir. Fred ain't too bad, but I fear Tom might not see the sun again.'

8

The moon gave Annabel sufficient light to find her way through the wicket gate in the hedge that bounded the kitchen garden. She had decided to scavenge there first as there should be a few tomatoes, salad leaves and some late raspberries on the canes. The orchard was the other side of the vegetable plot, it would be a simple task to slip in and gather a few apples to eat with whatever else she found.

It was full dark and she was expecting to hear sounds of the ambush coming from the house at any moment. She was far enough away to be out of danger even if shots were fired from within. The only drawback to her scheme was that she had to pass within twenty-five yards of the stable block and dreaded to think what *his* reaction would be if he discovered her creeping about like this.

She paused on seeing the black outline of the barn. Silence. Confident she could continue to collect her dinner by slipping from shadow to shadow, she continued. So busy listening she knocked an unwary boot against a pile of flowerpots sending them tumbling to the ground. The noise echoed in the darkness and instinctively she dropped to her hands and knees, hoping to remain undetected. She was not sure if she was more frightened of being heard by the colonel or by the intruders.

Slowly her heart stopped thudding in her ears; there had been no reaction from the house, no doors flung open, no running feet in her direction. Neither had there been any noise from the stables or barn. Thank God! Her carelessness had not attracted any unwanted attention so she could continue to forage for her supper. She remained crouched in the darkness for a further few minutes to be absolutely sure she was alone. Confident she could continue her journey, she straightened and stepped straight into a solid wall of flesh.

Her scream of shock was stifled by a rough hand clapped across her mouth. Too scared to struggle when something smelly was dragged over her head and she was lifted from her feet. Next, she was carried through the darkness slung over the shoulder of her captor. She couldn't breathe, was terrified her bladder would empty.

The jolting journey was over in moments and she was dumped unceremoniously to the ground. All this was done without a word being spoken. She had no idea if she was inside the hall or somewhere else entirely. If her abductor did not remove the noisome sack she would choke. Her nostrils were becoming blocked by dust and straw, her mouth already full of something similar. Was she to be left to suffocate?

Suddenly the material was snatched away. She tried to breathe, but her lungs were too full of debris, she choked and coughed, her chest a band of pain. Then she was upended and thumped hard between her shoulders, the force of the blows causing the blockage to be expelled.

Wheezing and gasping for breath, tears streaming down her cheeks, she believed she was dying. Then gentle fingers forced open her mouth and deftly removed the remaining straw.

'Take shallow breaths. Relax, your lungs are clear now, let nature take over.'

She did as instructed and slowly the restriction began to ease and her head cleared. Her nose was still blocked and she blew it noisily wiping away the mess with the sleeve of her jacket. As her breath calmed so her indignation grew. The colonel had almost killed her.

The man was deranged! He had deliberately treated her like an enemy in order to punish her for supposedly disobeying his orders. A tin mug was held to her lips and she drank thirstily. The water removed the last of the obstructions and when she'd finished she was more than ready to tell him exactly what she thought of his behaviour.

Before she could begin her tirade he squatted down beside her. 'God's teeth! My dear girl, you have a propensity for living dangerously. What the hell were you doing skulking about in the vegetable patch? I thought you were one of the intruders.' This was spoken in a harsh whisper.

'Why should you think that? I am in no way like one of the vagabonds. You must have realized who it was as soon as I walked into you.'

There was an ominous silence. 'It did not occur to me, Miss Bentley. I had given you a direct order, I am unused to having those ignored.'

She swallowed nervously. 'I did not come anywhere near the stables. I was going to get myself something to eat. If I had not trodden on the flowerpots you would never have known I was there.'

Another voice whispered from the darkness. 'The colonel heard you long before that, miss, he was out there waiting.'

'Billy!' Her exclamation was too loud and

immediately she was admonished. 'I'm sorry, Colonel Sinclair, but I was so pleased to hear his voice. How are you?'

'Fair to middling, miss. The major reckons I'll be well again in a day or so.'

This whispered conversation was brought to an abrupt halt by a sharp command. 'Be silent, both of you.'

She collapsed against the wall, too tired and dispirited to argue further. Although her lungs were working more or less normally every breath she took was painful. She didn't dare to clear her throat as she had already caused enough problems. Tears trickled unheeded down her face and she bit her lips trying to keep back her sobs. Too much had happened to her and her family in the past few hours.

Her beloved mother could have been found already, the monsters could be ... She gulped, she could not bear to think what might be happening inside the house. Dark memories of her stepfather flooded her mind.

There was a slight movement beside her and she was lifted, as if she weighed nothing, and carried across the barn. It was coal black, no glimmer of moonlight filtering in through the cracks in the wall, how could he march so confidently when he was moving blind?

'Don't cry, sweetheart. I'm a brute to treat

you so harshly. Let me hold you; you are shivering, my warmth shall soon restore you.' He folded, still holding her close, on to a convenient wooden box.

His words had been spoken softly into her ear, for her alone. She should protest. A well-brought up young lady would never allow herself to be comforted in this way, but she relaxed, as her terror and anxiety trickled away. Sighing she closed her eyes, it was so warm and comfortable cradled in his arms, it was as if she belonged there.

★ ★ ★

Robert felt the girl in his arms go limp, then waited a few more moments until her breathing became regular. Carefully regaining his feet, he twisted and placed her in the bed of straw he had prepared. After tucking his riding coat around her he stepped back satisfied she was safe. He cursed inwardly that his carelessness had almost killed her. He had been too long away from military service, his instincts no longer honed sharp. He would not have made such a mistake two years ago. Even after the tragedy he had remained clear-sighted and focused.

Maybe it was time to resign his commission, give up all thought of serving King and country; thirty was not old, he was in his prime. Dudley had the right idea, he was intending to join the East India Company, having only a small private income to live on. His friend had already resigned, it was time he did the same.

Gesturing it was time to leave, he moved to the exit and began to rebuckle his sword belt. The pistols were tucked into his coat pockets, handles protruding ready to be snatched out when needed. They were both loaded and primed, all he had to do was cock and fire.

'How are the men?' Dudley had been ministering to the injured whilst he had been on guard, and then taking care of the girl. He didn't trust himself to think of her as Annabel, it would make her too familiar; he had loved a woman once, would never allow himself to do so again.

'Billy and Fred are doing well; not so sure about Tom's chances of survival.'

'When this is over, we must send for a quack. Least we can do, seeing it was Billy who brought this disaster with him.'

Deftly wrapping his muffler back around his face, he jammed his hat down hard and was ready. Neither of them had stocks to remove, these were already in use as bandages. He gripped the edge of the door and pulled it open sufficiently for them to pass through. He stood for a moment letting his eyes adjust, it was far lighter out here, but moonlight could be deceptive, making innocent objects seem dangerous and vice versa.

In a half crouch he led the way round to the side of the house. There were glazed doors that opened on to the terrace and it was here he intended to effect an entry. 'Noise coming from the rear. They're in the kitchen. Makes it easier for us,' he hissed over his shoulder.

'Understood.'

He had worked so often with his friend there was little need for verbal communication.

As he'd hoped the doors leading into the drawing-room were only fastened by a catch. Pulling out the blade he kept in his boot top he slipped it into the gap and jiggled it around. The doors opened, he stepped inside and Dudley followed. Together they secured the catch behind them. The wind was getting up, it wouldn't do to risk the doors banging and alerting the intruders.

There was sufficient light from outside to show him the layout of the room. He ran, soft-footed, across to the entrance of the formal dining-room; it was from here he intended to begin his ambush. This chamber had a servant's exit that led directly to the kitchen, ideal for his purpose. They would not be expecting an attack to arrive from the interior of the house. It was remotely possible they might have someone watching the main doors, but not the direction from which he intended to come.

Easing the door open a fraction he put his ear to it; the sound of raucous laughter was coming from the kitchen, no evidence to suggest any of the men were on guard. This was going to be easier than he had anticipated. His pistols ready, he glanced over his shoulder to check Dudley was behind him.

He crept forwards keeping his back hard against the panelling, remembering to duck the beams that crossed the narrow passage. A thud followed by a muttered curse told him his friend had forgotten to do so. He froze, waiting to see if the small disturbance had alerted their quarry. No, the noise continued unabated.

It had been decided to disable rather than kill, if possible. Robert hoped their sudden appearance, faces muffled and armed to the teeth, would be enough to terrify their opponents into submission without having to fire their weapons. However, they had both agreed any sign of resistance would be dealt with harshly. These men had already murdered his driver and tried to kill the other three; if they weren't killed in the ambush they would certainly dance at the end of a rope.

He paused outside the kitchen door, he was to enter this way, Dudley from the scullery. He let four minutes pass as planned, counting the seconds in his head, and then slowly lifted the latch leaving the door open a fraction. He continued the count until he reached sixty and then erupted into the room with the major.

'Hands on the table. Remain where you are or you die.' His roared command had the desired effect and all six renegades slammed their hands down. They were looking certain death in the face, and knew it.

Keeping his cocked guns levelled at the largest man, and the one beside him, he stepped in behind the first and spun his pistol, then crashed it down on the back of the leader's head. The second man was dealt with, with equal efficiency. It had taken less than thirty seconds to dispatch these two and now the remaining four knew there was a bullet for each of them.

Dudley removed the twine, they had found in the barn, from his pocket and with both weapons aimed at the two men nearest to him he gestured to one. 'On your feet. Now. Hands behind your back. Do it.' His voice cracked like a whip and the men were too drunk and demoralized to put up any resistance.

With calm efficiency the six murderers were trussed up, gagged, and the four still on their feet, herded outside to be shoved into an empty loose box. Once inside it was the work of minutes to tie them ensuring they could not escape. The two unconscious men were dragged, one at a time, feet first to join their comrades. Robert slammed the bolt across leaving Dudley to fasten it with twine. There was no chance of the men escaping unless somebody undid the door for them.

'That was well done; reminded me of the Peninsula. We must get back inside and find the ladies.'

'At least the range is still alight; after handling that rabble I stink like a cesspit.' Dudley waved his hand in front of Robert. 'Good God! The stench is overpowering.'

Robert grinned, his teeth a flash of white in the darkness, and slapped him on the back. 'We make a good team, and we have smelt far worse than this. I don't want to disturb the girl until we know her mother's safe.'

'If they had been found Billy would have heard the screaming and mentioned it to us. They must be hiding.'

Robert delayed a few moments in order to

light a lantern. Their return journey was far easier when they could see. The back door was open, he decided to leave it like that, try and clear the noxious smell the intruders had left behind.

'I think the best way to go about this search is to stand in the central hall and shout; they should hear us,' Dudley suggested.

Several shouts from both of them elicited no response. 'They must be hiding in the attics, where they were when we first arrived. I doubt they can hear anything up there. I have no idea how to release the mechanism to the panel in the boot room. I shall have to fetch Miss Bentley after all.'

'You do that, I'll do my best to clean up the kitchen. I noticed they had drunk both bottles of brandy, and several of home-made wine. We shall be on short commons tonight.'

'It's a damn good job they did, it made our job all the easier.'

He was happy to leave the domestic duties to his friend, for some reason he was eager to hold the girl again.

★ ★ ★

Annabel jolted awake. Where was she? It was pitch dark and there was the sound of heavy breathing in the blackness. Sleep fogged her brain. She couldn't understand where she was or who was with her.

'Miss Bentley, are you awake?'

A rush of relief cleared her head. It was Billy's voice. She recalled everything including being cradled like a child on Sinclair's lap. It was too late too repine; propriety and etiquette had been abandoned long ago where that gentleman was concerned.

'Obviously, I am, Billy. How are you? Do you think it's all over? Did you hear anything whilst I was asleep?'

'Not a lot, miss, a deal of banging a bit earlier. I reckon those varmints are safely stored in a stable. I saw a light flickering so someone has lit a lantern.'

'In which case, I shall do the same for us. There's a tinderbox in the tack room if I can find it. I'm sure it would seem more cheerful with lanterns in here.' As she groped towards the door she heard heavy footsteps approaching. It must be either the colonel or Major Dudley, all the murderers were safely imprisoned, weren't they?

9

The door swung open and Colonel Sinclair stepped in, his lantern held aloft. 'Excellent. I was coming to fetch you, Miss Bentley. The house is secure but we are unable to access the secret passage and need your assistance.'

Annabel wanted to throw herself into his arms, but restrained her impulse. 'Thank you, Colonel. Billy said he had heard you disposing of the men. How many are dead?'

'Good God! What a bloodthirsty young lady you are; none of them. Two have sore heads, but the others are unharmed.'

'My mother and Mary are perfectly safe in the attics; I think it would be better if you concentrated your attention on getting poor Tom and Fred somewhere more comfortable.' She spoke without considering, as used to giving orders as he was. He ground his teeth.

'Yes, thank you for reminding me. I had of course forgotten all about the injured men.'

'I beg your pardon, sir, if I have caused offence. I am grateful to you and Major Dudley for riding to the rescue so ably. However, in case *you* had forgotten this is

Brandon Hall and here *I* am in charge.'

Billy spoke from the darkness. 'Fred is awake, sir, I reckon between us we could get him inside.'

'You must not exert yourself, Billy. If you can go ahead and fetch Mary and Lady Sophia down, then I am sure that the Colonel and I between us can bring Fred in.'

The young man appeared beside her. He glanced at the colonel, who nodded, before replying. 'Right you are, Miss Bentley. Fred showed me how the catch worked, I reckon I can still recall how to do it.'

'Here, lad, take the lantern. With the doors wide open we can see well enough in here.' He turned and stared down at her. 'Come along, Miss Bentley. I am yours to command.'

An irresistible desire to giggle overwhelmed her, she turned her back hoping to disguise her amusement. The tight hold made her jump, but she didn't attempt to step away.

'Miss Bentley, I am not used to being mocked.'

His words were soft, but did not fool her for a moment. He was too close, his heat burning through her clothes. Her throat was dry and a strange tingling began in the areas that were almost touching him. Her feet were stuck to the floor, the power of speech deserted her.

119

His fingers began to stroke the place he had held. The gap between them lessened and, unable to help herself, she leant against him. Instantly the hand on her shoulder slid down her arm to encircle her waist. Her knees, that had remained firm throughout the day, began to tremble. He spun her around until she was standing, loosely held, within his embrace.

'Look at me, sweetheart, I want to see your face.'

Slowly she tilted her head, not sure what was happening, but certain whatever it was she welcomed the experience. His arms tightened and suddenly her feet were floating and she was staring into his eyes. Her lips parted and a strange heat surged around her body. Then his mouth covered hers and she was lost, wanted something more from him, but was not sure what it was.

★   ★   ★

Robert wanted to crush her against him, explore every inch of her with his tongue and hands. His head was spinning — it was so long since he'd felt such passion. She was his for the taking, her breasts hard against him, her fingers tangling in his hair. From somewhere he found the strength to put her down and step away before it was too late. He was as shaken as she.

Her face was bemused, her eyes huge; even dressed as a boy she was the most desirable woman he had ever met. Was it possible he could love again after all?

'Miss Bentley, that was unpardonable. I most humbly apologize for behaving in such an ungentlemanly manner. I give my word it will not happen again.'

'It won't? Oh, well! It was a most enjoyable experience, and you have no need to beg my pardon, I was a willing participant.'

His shout of laughter echoed around the empty barn rousing Fred from his slumber. 'Is that you, Colonel Sinclair? I've got a right bad headache, I can tell you, nothing to laugh about.'

'I'm so glad you're awake. If the colonel and I help you, do you think you can manage the walk back to the house?'

'I reckon so, but it ain't a job for a lady. I'll wait until the major comes to help.'

'Miss Bentley, I think you must accept he's right. Dudley is cleaning up the kitchen — he would be better down here, and you replace him at his task.'

'I'll send the major to you; I'm sure there is an old door somewhere in here you could use to carry poor Tom into the house.'

121

She hurried out, apparently less affected by their lovemaking than he. He'd never met anyone like her, either male or female. It was going to be stimulating being in close contact with Annabel Bentley these next few days. He and Dudley had already decided to stay at Brandon Hall until Lady Sophia's staff were well enough to work and, judging by the parlous state of Tom, that could be some time. His guilt at his betrothed's untimely death was somehow less painful today. Had saving Annabel and her mother released him from the blackness?

★ ★ ★

Annabel burst into the kitchen to be greeted by cries of excitement. 'My darling girl, your heroics have saved our lives. I am so proud of you. You grow more like your father every month.'

'Mama, it was not me who captured the murderers, you must thank the colonel and the major for that.' She extricated herself from her mother's arms and turned to Mary. 'I am so sorry about Tom and Fred. I have been sent to fetch Major Dudley so that both of them can be brought inside.'

'Billy told us what happened, miss. Poor old Jethro, it weren't fair what happened to him. With God's good grace my Tom will pull through. I'm going to check those devils didn't get into our rooms. Is someone to go for the doctor?'

Dudley stepped round the three women. 'As soon as I have assisted the colonel with the transfer of your husband and son, Mrs Hopkins, I shall go to fetch him.'

The kitchen smelt appalling, but the windows were open and the stench would soon go. The kettle was hissing on the range, so Annabel would make everyone a hot drink. Tea was a precious commodity, but the caddie was not kept locked, there was no need at Brandon Hall to protect their possessions from misuse by the staff.

'My dear girl, might I suggest you take a jug of hot water upstairs to wash? Apart from mud and horsehair, you are also covered in straw.'

'It hardly seems worthwhile to change so late in the day, we shall all be retiring soon.' She frowned, remembering the major's promise to ride for the doctor. 'It would be better if neither of us were downstairs when the physician arrives. It might still be possible to keep our presence here a secret. The gentlemen can say they had come to visit Great-aunt Beth, only to find her . . . '

'Exactly! They can hardly tell him that

she's buried in the orchard. They don't have that information themselves. Perhaps it would be best to explain the whole; they are already so embroiled in our business it would make little difference to tell them everything.'

'So, are we to retire to our chambers or not?'

Her mother waved her arms and shrugged. 'I shall leave the decision to you, my love. You are so much better at that sort of thing than I am. Now, I am going into the scullery to see if there is anything left to eat, I am decidedly hungry and I have not been galloping all over the countryside. I imagine that you must all be faint from lack of food.'

Should they risk explaining their situation to the colonel and his friend? She felt a sudden pulse of heat at the thought of how much he already knew about her. She had allowed him to take liberties with her person. If her mother ever found out he would be obliged to make her an offer. He was not the kind of man she wished to marry, he was too dictatorial, too used to having his own way. However, the thought of being loved by him made her glow in a most inappropriate manner.

He was an attractive man who aroused feelings in her that were quite improper, but surely this was no basis for marriage? She paused — shocked by her imaginings. Robert was not just a handsome man, he was kind, intelligent and courageous. She clutched the door frame. How had this happened? She'd spent barely an hour in his company, but had the strangest suspicion her affections were engaged.

The sound of booted feet alerted her to the arrival of the first of the patients. The next half an hour was so busy there was no time to think about anything apart from making the two men comfortable. Tom was deeply unconscious, his breathing barely discernible, but Fred was quite lucid and able to walk with just an arm around his shoulders.

'There's supper in the kitchen, and I have a tray prepared for Fred. I have made soup, and there was a fresh loaf and cheese untouched.' Lady Sophia sighed. 'I'm afraid, Major Dudley, that your beautiful ham has been entirely demolished by the vagabonds.'

'I shall purchase another for you, my lady, when I ride for the doctor tomorrow morning.' He turned to speak to Mary who was fussing over the tray for her son. 'Are you quite sure, Mrs Hopkins, that you do not wish me to go tonight?'

'No, sir. I doubt there's little anyone can do. He's warm and comfortable; it's up to the good Lord to decide whether he lives or dies.'

Annabel's eyes filled. Mary was so brave to accept what had happened without complaint. If her mama had been struck down like Tom, she would have been distraught. And Robert? What if he'd been gravely injured? A wave of horror shook her; if anything happened to him she would be inconsolable.

'If there's anything at all that I can do to help you with the nursing, Mary, you must ask.'

'Heavens! Thank you, miss, but I can manage. It's not for the likes of you to look after my Tom or Fred. If you can help her ladyship with the cooking, that would be much appreciated.'

The domestic duties could be accomplished, it was the livestock and outdoor tasks that would be a problem. There wasn't enough money to hire any temporary staff, and it might be many weeks before Tom, or indeed Fred, were fit for duty. This realization made her next decision easy. The gentlemen must be told everything. It was possible there might be some sort of reward available for capturing the renegades. She trusted Robert's judgement; he was bound to know about that sort of thing. Her cheeks flushed. Had he now become Robert in her thoughts?

'Come along, my love, you shall feel better

when you have eaten. Then a good night's sleep is required to complete your recovery.'

The major offered to help serve the impromptu supper waving her away when she volunteered to take his place. 'No, my dear girl, you look exhausted. Sit down before you fall, and let me assist your mama.'

She slumped into a chair propping her head upon her hands, almost too tired to eat. A bowl of vegetable soap was placed in front of her and, when she inhaled the aromatic steam, her stomach rumbled loudly. Her hand refused to move and gentle fingers curled it round her spoon and guided the soup to her mouth. Like a child she swallowed the broth and immediately her hunger took over what *he* had started.

The soup slurped from spoon to mouth and was gone. She scraped around the empty dish. 'I'm still hungry, but that was the best soup I have ever eaten, Mama.'

'I could hear that you were enjoying it, my dear. Have some bread and cheese and one of the apples you picked yesterday.'

Annabel straightened and glanced around the table. What a mix of people were sitting there; a member of the aristocracy, a colonel and a major, a groom and the daughter of a captain. How revolutionary! It was only then she comprehended how extraordinary Brandon Hall had become. Mary, Tom and Fred were not just servants, but friends and the only family she had ever known apart from her mother.

Her eyes drifted towards the man who had awakened something inside her. He was unaware of her scrutiny, munching his way through bread and cheese like his life depended on it. Then, to her horror he looked at her, his mouth twitched into a lopsided smile that sent her heart cartwheeling. Her eyes immediately returned to her food.

No longer hungry, she replaced her cutlery, drank the last of her tea and addressed her mother. 'If you don't mind, Mama, I'm almost asleep on my feet. I'm going to retire before someone is obliged to carry me up the stairs.' Pushing herself upright was almost too much for her.

Both gentlemen were on their feet, Billy didn't move, he had nodded off where he sat.

'Goodnight, Miss Bentley. We have much to discuss, but it can wait until the morning.'

'We do, Colonel. Goodnight everyone.' She stopped; there was something everyone had overlooked. 'I am not sure if the two rooms you used last time have been prepared . . . '

'I shall take care of that, my love, I know where the linen is kept. I shall come up with you, and bring the hot water, I don't think you are in a fit state to carry it yourself.'

Too late to prevent the inevitable from happening, Annabel stood by helplessly as the colonel relieved her mother of her burden. 'Allow me, my lady. If you lead the way, I shall follow. There's no necessity for you to do any more than find us what we need. Dudley and I are quite able to take care of ourselves.'

At least if he was carrying the hot water he could not snatch her up. Halfway up the stairs she almost wished she was being carried, her legs were heavy and her feet seemed determined to go in a different direction to the one she required. She leant against the balustrade; she had ridden twenty miles, surely a few stairs would not defeat her now.

From a distance she heard the murmur of voices and then well remembered arms swung her up and she settled her head against him with a sigh of contentment. Too soon her mother was directing him to place her down and he had gone from her bedchamber.

'Sit up, darling, and I shall undress you like I used to when you were small.'

Obediently she raised and lowered her arms and feet when instructed and submitted uncomplaining when she was thoroughly washed.

'There you are, child, that is the best I can do tonight. You must have a bath in the morning.'

'I have decided, we must tell them everything. We cannot manage here on our own without help.'

'Don't fret about it now, get some sleep, tomorrow is soon enough to explain why we must remain invisible here.'

Annabel was asleep before her mother had left the room and did not stir until the sound of horses approaching roused her from her slumbers.

10

Instantly alert, Annabel tumbled out of bed and ran across to her window. The shutters had not been closed and early morning sunlight streamed into her chamber. She pressed herself against the edge of the window and looked down. Oh no! It was the militia; too late, she recalled the colonel telling her he would send for them. They were already halfway down the drive; she did not have long to save her mother and herself from disaster.

Why hadn't she explained to him their circumstances? Frantically she grabbed the first gown on the rail in her closet, the requisite undergarments, and began to dress. Ten minutes later her hair more or less coiled around her head she was ready to descend. It was vital that she spoke to the colonel before he met the militia.

It was barely dawn and she prayed that he was still in his room and not already downstairs. She banged on his door and was relieved to hear his voice bid her enter. She remained in the doorway hoping this would be enough to save her from her mother's wrath. Young ladies never entered a gentleman's bedchamber under *any* circumstances.

'Colonel Sinclair, I have to speak to you most urgently. The militia are here and before you go down to see them there is something you must know. I shall wait for you in the gallery, please do not be long.' She had barely marshalled her thoughts when he was beside her.

'What is it that I must know?'

'Do you remember how shocked I was when you mentioned Sir Randolph Rushton?' He nodded. 'He is my stepfather. Nearly four years ago Mama and I fled from his house and have been hiding here ever since. He is a dreadful man, I cannot speak of the things he did, but we shall both be in jeopardy if he ever discovers where we are living.'

'I had already guessed most of this; Rushton is not received by decent families. His reputation is well known.' His brow creased and his eyes half closed. 'I shall tell them half the truth, that Dudley and I came here by chance, and when we heard of the attack felt obligated to come to the rescue.'

'There is more that I have to tell you. We came here to live with Great-aunt Beth, a relative on Mama's side of the family, but she was already bedridden when we arrived. When she died a few months later, at her insistence she was buried in the orchard. Her will has never been read, and it is on *her* annuity that we are living.' Annabel stared up at him willing him to understand. 'If we had announced her death, involved the lawyers and the clergy, the fact that Mama was her beneficiary would become common knowledge.'

'I understand perfectly. However, it does complicate matters slightly. Don't look so worried, sweetheart, I shall take care of things.' He raised a hand but let it fall again without touching her. 'I promise you, that bastard shall never get his hands on either of you whilst I have breath in my body.'

She shivered involuntarily. Although his anger was not directed at her, his expression frightened her. 'Please, go down and talk to the militia before they wake the household. If Mary answers the door she will not have the same story as you.'

There was nothing more she could do, it was up to him now. She drifted back to her own apartment to wait until the military had gone, certain he would smooth things over. Her lips curved. Having someone to turn to for help was a blessing, it was a most welcome state of affairs.

★   ★   ★

133

It was as he'd suspected, Lady Sophia had been abused by Rushton. Although society might blame her for abandoning her marriage, he did not. No lady should be obliged to suffer at the hands of a man. If she had no family to support her there had been no choice. She must have considered her daughter to be at risk from him and that was why she had left when she did.

He was committed to keeping them both safe and if this meant he was obliged to marry Annabel, then so be it. He had given his word as a gentleman to protect her. Maria would understand the necessity to break his vow of celibacy. It did not occur to him to offer a marriage in name only.

God's teeth! Dudley was there before him and had already gone out to speak to the militia captain. He took the last flight of stairs in one jump and crossed the hall at a run. The red-coated soldiers had dismounted and their officer was deep in conversation with his friend.

'Major Dudley, a word if you please.' His barked command sent the horses skittering and in the confusion he was able to grab the major's arm and move him to one side. 'Dudley, have you mentioned Lady Sophia and Miss Bentley?'

'Of course I have, why wouldn't I? Captain

Jenkins asked who was the owner of Brandon Hall and I saw no reason not to tell him.'

'This is an unmitigated disaster. Miss Bentley has just confirmed what we suspected — Lady Sophia *is* the runaway wife of that bastard Rushton we were talking about with your sister. They have been hiding here for years, and now it is inevitable that their whereabouts will become common knowledge.'

'My God! How could I have forgotten? This is all my doing. I cannot retract the information; the whole troop overheard what I said.'

'What else did you tell them?'

'Nothing of importance, just the facts of the case. I have only been out here a few minutes.'

Robert could think of only one thing that might prevent Sir Randolph arriving at Brandon Hall demanding his wife and daughter return with him. He strode to the captain. 'I am Colonel Sinclair.'

Instantly the man jumped to attention and his troop followed suit, the sound of clicking heels sent a flock of pigeons whirling into the air in protest. 'Captain Jenkins at your service, sir. A bad business, but it could have been far worse but for you and Major Dudley.'

'Exactly so. I am recently betrothed to Miss Bentley, I am frequently here.' He heard his friend cough behind him at this unexpected news. 'Major Dudley and I were visiting Brandon Manor when a stable lad came to fetch us. The six renegades are trussed and locked in a stable. I shall leave you to dispose of them.'

'We have been searching for these men for weeks, Colonel, I shall be more than happy to remove them.'

'Major Dudley, show Captain Jenkins where they are. I must return to reassure the ladies.'

Ramrod stiff he marched into the house wondering exactly how he was going to explain to Lady Sophia that he was now engaged to be married to her spirited daughter. They had been acquainted barely a week, not long, but quite long enough to know she would not take kindly to the news.

Perhaps the best way to approach this delicate matter was to emphasize the fact that he was preferable to Sir Randolph. Yes, that should win the first skirmish, but he doubted it would win the battle. There were plans to make and he needed somewhere quiet to do this. The library would be ideal.

The room was obviously well used, a fire laid ready to light. He preferred to think on his feet and began to pace the length of the room. How long would it be before someone sent Rushton the news that his wife was hiding in Suffolk? Until today neither Dudley nor himself had known for certain she was Lady Sophia Rushton which meant she might not be identified directly.

Two weeks — with luck the news would not reach London any quicker. Was that enough time to send for reinforcements from his estate in Hertfordshire? He employed several veterans and they would be ideal to deter Rushton from attempting to snatch his wife or stepdaughter. He must also discover the nearest bishop and obtain a marriage licence, Annabel would have to be his wife before her stepfather arrived.

He paused. There was something missing from this, but what was it? God's teeth! His machinations would only protect Annabel, Rushton could still legally demand the return of his wife. There was only one man who could protect Lady Sophia and that was her father. He must be an earl at least, or she would not use the title in this way. Surely he could be persuaded to intervene?

Decisions made, Robert headed for the rear of the house. In all the excitement he had neglected to enquire how the patients were doing. Dudley would have to ride for a doctor as soon as the militia had been dealt with.

★ ★ ★

Annabel watched proceedings from her window. Colonel Sinclair spoke only briefly to the militia officer before returning to the house. She prayed he had been in time, if he hadn't they would have to move, find somewhere else to hide. Her mother rarely appeared before late morning, but this was one occasion it was imperative she was roused immediately.

Perhaps a jug of hot chocolate would make the shock of seeing an early morning less painful. Mary was busy in the kitchen making bread and looked remarkably cheerful. 'How is Tom? From your expression I'm assuming he has improved overnight.'

'Yes, he woke up a while ago, he's not making much sense, but his colour's better. I reckon as he'll pull through.'

'I'm so glad. I must tell you the militia are here. I doubt that they will come in and speak to you, but if they do remember not to mention either myself or Mama.'

'I know better than that, miss. The colonel's already inside. He's somewhere downstairs.'

138

'I shall speak to him later on. I have come to make Mama a breakfast tray — is there any chocolate left?'

'Lawks a mussy! The varmints didn't find that, thank the good Lord. Shall I do it for you?'

'No, you get on with your tasks. It will be a relief to have the prisoners removed from here.'

With a tray upon which were a jug of chocolate, freshly baked rock cakes and two plates and cups, Annabel headed for her mother's chamber. She was obliged to balance her burden on one arm in order to open the door but managed it without spilling anything.

'Mama, I have brought us breakfast. I must talk to you immediately.'

The room was dark, the shutters closed. It was difficult to pick her way through the clutter on the floor to find a clear surface on which to put the tray. By the time this was accomplished the mound under the comforter was stirring.

'Good gracious, Annabel, what dire emergency has brought you here so early?' This first remark was followed by a second, more urgent. 'Oh dear! Is it Tom? Has he died? How dreadful, I shall come at once.'

'No, Mama, Tom is much better this

morning. It is something else entirely.' She threw open the shutters flooding the room with autumn sunlight. 'There, now I can see enough to avoid tripping over.'

The chocolate was still piping hot, the rock cakes warm from the oven and the rich smell filled the room. 'Heavenly! Bring mine over, darling girl, I find myself almost pleased at being woken at this ungodly hour.'

Annabel waited until they had both eaten before explaining why she had to come.

'We must hope that the colonel was able to smooth things over. If our names were mentioned in the report it is certain Rushton will hear of it. God knows what we should do then. We have nowhere else to go, and no money to live on if we do.'

'What about Great-aunt Beth's will? If we are discovered then we can have it read . . . ' Her voice faltered. 'Of course, until we have a death certificate we cannot do that either.'

'I must get up at once. We have to speak to Major Dudley; he will give us good advice, I'm sure of that.'

Major Dudley? Why had her mother not said Colonel Sinclair? He was the senior party, surely he was the one they must refer to? Her lips twitched. In fact the colonel was several years younger than his friend, it was just that he outranked him and behaved as if he was in charge of events.

'I shall leave you to get ready. The colonel knows all about the orchard. I must change into my work clothes and go and see to the livestock. We cannot expect our guests to do all the outside work for us.'

'You must stay as you are, Annabel. Put on an apron and cap. I am not happy to have you parading around in men's clothes today.'

She left her mother to get dressed and hurried back to the kitchen with the tray. Mary was in the scullery and she took it directly to her. 'I'm going out to milk the cow and feed the fowl. I hope, with an apron and cap on, even if I am seen by the militia they will just think me a serving girl.'

'I reckon they'll be gone soon. There's been a deal of shouting and carrying on alarming out there these past twenty minutes. I could do with some more eggs, if there are any, miss.'

Annabel found the things she required on the shelf in the boot room and quickly put them on. Slipping out, she walked briskly towards the meadow in which the house cow was lowing miserably. Poor thing, it was way past her usual milking time. She collected a halter and ran to the field. 'Never mind, Buttercup, did you think we had forgotten you? Come along, I shall take you to the dairy

141

and make you comfortable once more.'

This cow had been at Brandon Hall several years, and produced a fine calf every other year. They had two heifers in the field, both in calf, but they would not give birth till the spring and didn't need milking.

In the dairy, Annabel tethered Buttercup to an iron ring, pulled up the stool, placed the milking pail correctly and began the chore. It took two hours to finish in the dairy and collect the eggs. There was no sign of anyone outside, so she checked the stables. The horses had been fed and watered, their loose boxes already mucked out.

She deposited the basket of eggs and jug of cream in the kitchen and went back to her room via the back stairs, not wishing to meet the colonel with her feet liberally coated with cow dung. The water in her jug was cold but perfectly adequate. For some reason this morning she wanted to look her best. She had thrown her clothes on anyhow when she'd risen in such a hurry, but now she was at leisure to select something a little more flattering than the ancient gown she was wearing.

There were not many items to choose from, sartorial elegance was not high on her list of priorities. What little money there was went in keeping the house warm and the occupants well fed. The only reason her mother had more flattering items to wear was because they had discovered several bales of material hidden in the attics.

Mama was an expert seamstress and made up her own clothes. However, Annabel did not expect her garments to be made in this way. As she was no expert with the needle herself, the best she could do was lengthen and adapt what she already owned.

Her fingers lingered on the one gown that was new. It had been her last name day gift. It was a deep blue muslin with a small white flower woven into the material. There had been no occasion to wear it until now. Mama had sent Fred to sell two of her pretty watercolours in Ipswich in order to pay for the cloth. Yes! Today was the right time. Being dressed in her finest would help her deal with whatever calamities might have arisen.

There was no time to wait for a bath to be drawn. She stripped off to stand naked on a linen square whilst she scrubbed herself from top to toe. Satisfied she was clean and no longer reeked of the farmyard, she stepped into her chemise and petticoats. Like all her gowns this one buttoned at the front and did not require the services of a maid to fasten it.

The dress had a fitted bodice, a moderately low neckline, and fell from directly under her bosom in a style that her mother had seen in a copy of *La Belle Assemblée*. This magazine had been purchased by Fred for her mother's anniversary. It was somewhat out of date, but Annabel felt in the first stare of fashion as she gazed wide-eyed in the mirror.

It suited her slenderness to perfection. The colour matched her eyes, and the darker blue silk of the sash which tied to one side, added the finishing touch. She even had blue slippers. They were not a perfect match, but anything was preferable to her boots.

She twirled, loving the way the material flowed around her body, knowing she was decidedly improper not to be wearing a corset. She didn't own one of these instruments of torture, so there was little she could do about it. Mama had once shown her the contraption and she couldn't imagine why any woman should wish to be laced up so tight they couldn't breathe. No wonder debutantes had a tendency to swoon in a press of people.

Certain she looked her best, she ran back along the passage, stopping at the gallery to peep over. There were voices downstairs coming from the drawing-room. Mama and both gentlemen were there and the talk was somewhat animated. Mama's voice was particularly agitated.

She gathered up her skirts and, with one hand lightly resting on the balustrade, she hurried down. Her mother did not sound worried or upset, more angry — what could have happened to make her cross?

11

In the drawing-room Major Dudley was looking decidedly uncomfortable, Colonel Sinclair furious and her mother white with rage. Her stomach roiled and she wished she hadn't eaten so many cakes at breakfast. The conversation stopped and all three stared at her.

'Mama, whatever is wrong? I could hear raised voices from upstairs.'

'Annabel, my dear girl, I have some appalling news for you.' Her mother shook her head. She turned. 'In fact, I have *two* equally appalling pieces of news to give you. You had better be seated, my love, whilst I tell you.'

Annabel had no intention of being the only one obliged to look up, so remained where she was. 'I am waiting, Mama. Please tell me at once what has disturbed you.'

Her mother flicked the colonel with a look of icy disdain. It must be something to do with what had happened between the colonel and herself. How could her mother know about the stolen kiss? Whatever he wasn't, Sinclair was a gentleman and would never have revealed what had transpired between them. Could she be mistaken?

'It would seem, my love, that Major Dudley, quite inadvertently I might add, revealed our names to the militia captain.'

Annabel's hands flew to her mouth. 'Good grief! We shall have to flee again. How long do we have, do you think, before *he* arrives on our doorstep demanding that we return with him?'

Her mother waved her silent. 'There is more to come. Colonel Sinclair has decided he must marry you in order to keep you safe. I can hardly believe he has had the temerity to suggest such an outrageous thing.'

He looked as though he was about to explode with anger. His jaw was clenched, his eyes black with rage.

'Mama, I think this is a matter that the colonel and I should discuss together. Is it not bad manners to mention such private things in public?'

It was as though she had slapped her mother. Lady Sophia deflated, her anger gone, and looked from one to another in bewilderment. 'Oh dear! You are quite right to reprimand me. How could I have been so gauche? I shall go to my room. I beg your pardon Major Dudley, I should never have spoken so forcefully in front of you.'

Annabel noticed her mother did not apologize to the colonel or retract what she had said. She wanted to follow, offer comfort and reassurance, but the major went instead. The door closed behind them, but she could hear the soft murmur of voices outside the door.

She needed to sit down. What had possessed the colonel to say they were to be married? She tottered to the nearest chair and collapsed, grateful her legs had been able to carry her that far. She didn't dare look to see what he was doing. His fury would no doubt be directed at her now her mother had fled the scene.

The sound of a chair being moved gave away his direction, and then he was sitting beside her, no more than a hand's breadth away.

'My dear girl, that was a horrible experience for you. I promise you I had spoken to your mother privately, but Major Dudley came in when he heard the raised voices.'

'It doesn't matter what you said, Colonel Sinclair. My mother was extremely rude. She did not appreciate the sacrifice you are prepared to make on our behalf.' She gripped the arms of the chair and pushed herself upright, his face was barely an inch from hers. Too close. Her pulse accelerated. She glowed all over. He observed her reaction and instantly moved his chair back a yard allowing her room to breathe.

'Miss Bentley, I have thought about this very carefully. As soon as I realized your whereabouts had been revealed to Captain Jenkins, it was quite clear what I had to do. I gave you my word that I would protect you, that I would not allow you to be snatched back by that bastard.' He looked at her directly, his expression strange, his eyes no longer black but navy-blue. They mesmerized her. 'I told Captain Jenkins that we were visiting here because you are my betrothed. I had no alternative, please understand that. We must be married before your stepfather arrives or he will be able to take you legally and only force will stop him.'

She swallowed as her breakfast threatened to return. 'You mean you would have to kill him?'

'I do. Believe me, I would not hesitate to do so. But that would not help me, or Lady Sophia or yourself.'

'I do not wish anyone else to be killed. Your driver has already met his end, that must be enough. I do understand what you are saying. I cannot believe that you would offer to give up your freedom to me. Good heavens, sir, we've only known each other five minutes. How can you be sure that we should suit?' She blushed.

'My dear, many marriages begin in this way. I'm certain in time we shall be completely comfortable together. By the time the babies come . . . ' As soon as he had spoken he regretted it. He had committed a grave error of judgement. She was staring at him in horror. He had made a complete mull of things. He kept forgetting she was a total innocent, had as much knowledge of what went on between a man and woman as a babe in arms.

'I beg your pardon, Miss Bentley. I should not have mentioned something so indelicate.' God's teeth! He'd done it again. Every time he opened his mouth he put his foot in it.

With great dignity she rose to her feet staring at him with such hauteur it made him feel like a schoolboy caught in a misdemeanour by the headmaster.

'Colonel Sinclair, I thank you most sincerely for your kind offer, but I must refuse. My mother and I have managed thus far, I'm sure we shall continue to do so without requiring you to take such a drastic step.'

He didn't blame her. What lovely young

woman would wish to marry a foul-mouthed soldier?

'I think you will find, my dear, you have no alternative. Without my support you will be dragged back to London and be at the mercy of your stepfather. I'm sure you know he treated your mother brutally. He will do the same to you if given the opportunity.'

'Sir, I should prefer to take my chances in that respect, rather than spend a life without love.' She raked him from head to toe and found him wanting. Then, with a toss of her head, she marched across the room.

The door was too far away. Annabel prayed she would reach it without tripping over her hem, or collapsing in an ignominious heap on the carpet. She was one step from safety when two arms slammed past her, trapping her between the door and his chest. Her head spun from his closeness, his particular aroma, of lemon soap and leather, flooded her nostrils.

'I didn't give you permission to leave. We have not finished our conversation, Miss Bentley.'

'Let me go at once, I wish to return to my chamber.'

The restraining arms vanished, she sighed with relief, but as she was about to take the final step he transferred his grip to her. She was turned to face him. He lifted her from the ground until her eyes were level with his. Her heart was pounding, a strange heat flooding through her body, what was happening to her? Was she unwell?

He drew her closer until her breasts were pressed hard against his shirt front. He removed one arm and encircled her waist, then with the other clasped her head and tilted it. She opened her mouth to protest, to demand that she was released at once, but her words were swallowed. His mouth covered hers in a kiss of such intoxicating sweetness she forgot everything else.

She was swept away on a sea of pleasure to a place she did not know existed. Of their own volition, her hands wound around his neck, to bury themselves in his hair. His lips were firm, she tasted the very essence of him, then something hot and moist slid across her mouth pushing her teeth apart. If she had still been on her feet this invasion would have been too much for her.

She didn't know what was happening, what he was doing. She was sure it was something her mother would not approve of. It was over as suddenly as it had begun. She was dropped on her feet and he was the other side of the room, staring across the park, breathing heavily, his back turned against her.

Without the door to lean on she would have been unable to stand. Her limbs felt heavy, a strange languor settled in a most unusual place. Why had he abandoned her? Had she done something to offend him? She was sure young ladies were not supposed to be kissed in that fashion, that it was something that could only happen between married couples. No sooner had the word popped into her head than she understood why he'd done it.

She understood why he'd talked of children. He did not love her, nor truly want a wife, but he desired her. That was surely better than indifference?

'Colonel Sinclair, have I upset you in some way? Should I not have kissed you back?'

He answered, but his voice seemed strange, as if he was in pain. 'I shall be all right in a moment. Sit down, sweetheart. There are many things we need to talk about.'

She subsided into the same chair she had occupied a few moments earlier. It was a *fait accompli*. She had no option now, she *had* to marry him. She had allowed him access to her person in a way that could not be acceptable unless they were betrothed. She blinked furiously to keep the tears at bay. This was not how it was meant to be. It had never been her intention to marry, she knew what

153

that led to. She wished to stay with Mama, live her life without interference from any man.

All this had changed in the space of a week. Two gentlemen from London had blundered into their lives and now she was engaged to be married to a virtual stranger. How could she bear it? There was movement on the far side of the room and she hastily dried her eyes on her skirt, rearranging it to cover the damp patch. She must be strong. Without this marriage Mama would be taken back and subjected to the most awful treatment. It is up to her to save them both.

'Annabel — no, don't look like that. It is quite permissible for me to use your given name now that we're engaged to be married. You must call me Robert.'

'I'm not sure if I can — this is a marriage of convenience, is it not? Perhaps when I know you better, I will feel more comfortable. Until then, I shall address you as before.' This refusal did not please him. Well, if he was to be her husband the sooner he realized she was not going to be browbeaten into submission the better.

'You must suit yourself, but I am not to be deterred. There are things that must be done and this is the first of them.'

To her utter astonishment he dropped to

one knee and with a commendably straight face clutched both hands to his heart in what she believed to be a parody of a lovesick suitor. 'My dearest Annabel, would you do me the inestimable honour of becoming my wife? Please make me the happiest of men by accepting my proposal.'

'Sinclair, kindly get up. You are making a cake of yourself. I'm not in the mood for levity.' For a dreadful moment she thought she had mortally offended him, that his proposal had been in earnest. Then he raised his head and his eyes blazed into hers.

'I'm not famous for my humour, my love. However, if you do not wish to be asked in this ridiculous manner, I shall desist.' He straightened, smiling down at her and she responded.

'As you have asked me so prettily, sir, I shall accept.' She sobered. 'I think it is a decision that we might both live to regret. We have nothing in common and in the short space of time that we have been acquainted we have spent most of it in argument.' Her cheeks blazed as she recalled what else they had spent their time doing.

'Exactly.' He picked up a similarly uphol-stered chair and, one-handed, positioned it opposite hers. 'Sweetheart, do you have any inkling of what shall be expected of you after

155

we're wed?' She shook her head, embarrassed by his question. 'I thought not. Your mother has been remiss in not explaining matters to you. Might I respectfully suggest that you ask her to remedy this omission immediately?'

How dare he criticize her mother? Her anger gave her the courage to look at him. 'This is not an acceptable topic of conversation, I shall not reply to your impertinent question.'

'In which case I shall move on. I intend to send to Hertfordshire and have my staff transfer here. This house cannot be run as it is.'

'Surely it would be far simpler if Mama and I removed there?' This was the answer. Even if Sir Randolph discovered their whereabouts by the time he arrived they could be elsewhere.

'God's teeth! My wits are wandering. That is the perfect solution. I shall not have to apply for a special licence and once under my roof I defy any man to remove you.'

'The only drawback to this plan is the fact that we cannot leave Mary on her own here, neither can we depart until your coachman has been buried.' She hesitated before continuing, 'Also, could I *respectfully* request that you desist from sprinkling blasphemies throughout your conversation?'

156

It was his turn to flush. 'I beg your pardon, my dear. As you have no doubt worked out for yourself I am a rough military man, little used to drawing-rooms and the company of ladies.'

Her laughter filled the room. 'That's doing it too brown, sir. You are more familiar with society than I am. I might have been cloistered in the country these past four years, but do know Wellington's officers were expected to attend the highest social functions.'

He grinned. It made him look younger, more approachable. '*Touché*, my love. But back to serious matters, I have already got the burial in hand. Dudley is going to call on the vicar whilst fetching the doctor.'

Suddenly his hands clenched and he swore volubly under his breath. She waited until he had stopped not daring to remonstrate this time. 'Colonel, what is it? Why are you so angry?'

'My carriage is still in pieces. Fred had not completed the repairs, and with him laid low they will not be done anytime soon. And if it was, two of my carriage horses are still at Brandon Manor, we would be unable to use it. We cannot leave Brandon Hall that way.'

He looked bleak and her throat clenched in fear. He did not have to explain it to her:

without the carriage they were trapped and at the mercy of her stepfather.

'Don't look so worried, little one. We shall come about, never fear. Let me think for a moment. Yes, I have it. We have a sen'night's grace, ample time for me to ride to Norwich and obtain a licence. We shall be married in the local church as soon as I return.'

'So soon? Is there no other way? Maybe you could ask Major Dudley if we could borrow his sister's carriage, Brandon Manor is not so far away as Norwich. If he set off as soon as he returns from the village he could be there this afternoon and return tomorrow morning.'

'And what if the carriage is not available? I should have wasted two days.' He stood up. 'My mind is made up, I shall go and speak to Lady Sophia and tell her what is going to happen.'

He strode off without another word and Annabel was unsure what had been decided. Whatever it was, there was work to be done and she could not sit around any longer in her best gown as if she was a lady of leisure. In the privacy of her chamber she came to her own decision. As soon as the colonel left for Norwich she and her mother would leave for Hertfordshire. Major Dudley could accompany them, that would leave just the

158

pony and livestock to feed, and Mary could manage that.

Buoyed up by the ingenuity of her plan she hurried down to the small parlour to find her mother and give her the good news.

12

'What the devil do you want? I thought I told you not to interrupt me?'

The footman shifted uneasily and held out a silver salver upon which there was a single letter. 'This arrived for you, sir, by express just now. I thought you needed to see it right away.'

Sir Randolph threw down his pen in disgust. 'Very well, bring it over. Don't stand there like an imbecile waving the tray where I can't reach it.'

Reluctantly the young man shuffled closer. 'Now, get out.' Impatiently he tore it open. His hand trembled and the colour in his face came and went. At last! After almost four years he'd found them. He'd never stopped looking, knew that one day they would make a mistake and reveal where they were living.

He spread the sheet of paper out on the desk and read it again more slowly.

Dear Sir Randolph,
I am writing to you with important news. I heard today that there had been an attack at Brandon Hall, Suffolk and a Lady

Sophia and a Miss Bentley were residing there. This report was given in a local newspaper. I am including the cutting with this note.

I look forward to your instructions on this matter. I remain your obedient servant,

yours respectfully
William Squires.

Brandon Hall? He'd never heard of it, how the devil did Sophia and Annabel come to be living there? Never mind, they could have no notion he was still looking for them, probably believed they were safe from his wrath. He was about to prove them wrong.

He looked again and swore viciously. There was no date on the letter, Squires was another imbecile. Why was he surrounded by incompetents and fools? Good God! He paid them enough. Why couldn't the people who served him give him what he required? He was tempted to screw the paper up and hurl it into the fire. The cutting; Squires had said there was a notice from the newspaper included with the letter. Surely that would have a date on it? He scrabbled through the debris on the desk but there was no sign of a piece of newsprint. Thoroughly enraged by another example of dereliction of duty, he tore the letter into shreds and scattered it across the floor.

He kicked his chair back enjoying the crash it made as it tumbled to the floor. He began to pace the carpet, but paused to admire his reflection in the over-mantel mirror. He raised his hand to push a lock of black hair back from his forehead. He doubted if his wife had aged as well as he. Annabel; now *she* was different. His eyes gleamed as he remembered the last time he'd seen her, so fresh and innocent, so sweetly rounded in all the important places.

A thrill of anticipation surged through his veins; it was to get his hands on his stepdaughter that he had spent so much time and money looking for the two of them. His wife could go to the devil, she had never been a willing partner. Even thrashing her had become routine, had not given him any pleasure.

★ ★ ★

'Dudley?' Robert's shout reverberated around the empty stable yard. He checked the loose box, the hunter his friend had ridden the previous day was missing. Dudley had already left on his errands. Dammit! That meant he would have to go in and speak to Lady

Sophia, explain his plans to her. He thought she was as easy to talk to as a bag of snakes. He grinned. He must learn to like her, after all she was to be his mother-in-law in four days' time.

He searched the main reception rooms with no luck, so headed to the rear of the house, to the small parlour he and Dudley had used on their previous visit. He tapped politely on the door and waited for a response. He was asked to enter.

'I beg your pardon for interrupting you, Lady Sophia, I had intended to talk to Dudley, but he has already left. I'm afraid I must talk to you instead.' Good God! He was at it again, feet first into any conversation.

Carefully she put away her embroidery frame and waved him towards a chair on the opposite side of the room, in front of the crackling fire. 'Please sit down, to have someone so formidable looming over one is a trifle overpowering.'

He took the chair she indicated and cleared his throat. 'Lady Sophia, I have spoken to Annabel, and she has done me the honour of accepting my offer of marriage.' He waited for the explosion.

'Major Dudley has explained it all to me. Colonel Sinclair, I was not fully cognizant of the sacrifice you're making on my daughter's

163

behalf. It is a splendid offer, and I am most grateful. Now I shall be sanguine that Annabel is safe, whatever happens to me in the future.'

'Excellent. I am setting off right away for Norwich, to find a bishop and get a licence so that we may be married as soon as possible. I had intended to ask Dudley to speak to the vicar on my behalf, but could you do so instead? I shall be back by Saturday, I want the vicar at the church at five o'clock that afternoon.'

She raised her eyebrows slightly and he realized he was being too abrupt. 'Beg your pardon, my lady. I am eager to leave, time is wasting. There is something else that I wish you to do for me.' He stared at her, not sure how to put this delicately. 'Annabel is an innocent, she appears totally ignorant of what is required of her once we are wed. Most girls of her age would already know these facts. Can you assure me that my intended will understand her duties by the time I return?'

She raised her head and smiled sweetly. 'Thank you so much, Colonel Sinclair, for pointing out that I have been remiss in *my* duties as a parent. It is so kind of you to take the trouble. I can assure you that this omission will be remedied by Saturday.' She stood up gracefully, and stared pointedly at the door.

He knew himself to be dismissed. He ground his teeth, holding back the pithy retort. 'In which case, madam, I shall take my leave. I have already said my farewells to Annabel.' He was halfway to the door when she called him back.

'Colonel Sinclair, I forgot to mention that Major Dudley is going to find some extra staff to help run Brandon Hall whilst Tom and Fred are indisposed. There ought to be plenty of local men glad to have the work; unemployment is rife in the countryside, as I'm sure you are aware.'

He waited, supposing it a rhetorical question. The lady frowned at his lack of response. Hastily he answered. 'Yes, indeed I am. An excellent notion, ma'am. I hope he will also employ indoor help for Mrs Hopkins.'

She nodded. 'He also said, and I hope he was not presumptuous in so doing, that as you are now engaged to Annabel, you will be quite happy to take responsibility for the added expense.'

'Of course I will, Dudley is quite correct. Do whatever you like, Lady Sophia. I have deep pockets and am happy to spend it on either yourself or Annabel. Things are going to be different around here, you shall not have to scrimp and save in future.'

She smiled, this time her eyes sparkled and she looked scarcely older than Annabel. 'Major Dudley assured me you are a gentleman, sir.' She hesitated, a faint flush stained her cheeks and then she looked him directly in the eye. 'As we have agreed, Annabel is still young in some respects for her years, I hope you are not expecting too much from her. She is unused to gentlemen of any sort, and you are scarcely well acquainted.'

He ran his finger around his stock which had become unaccountably tight. 'Exactly. Now the war is over, I'm hoping I can take Annabel abroad, if that is what she would like. I've no intention of setting up my nursery for a good few years yet.'

She nodded, satisfied with his answer. 'Thank you, Colonel Sinclair. I knew I could rely on you. Now, Godspeed. Major Dudley will take care of us in your absence.'

Why was Major Dudley being mentioned so often? Good God! Lady Sophia was smitten with his friend. He bowed and left the room thinking about this sad state of affairs. Whilst Sir Randolph lived there was no hope for *that* relationship. He stopped. He hoped his friend had not decided to dispatch his rival, and thus gain the hand of the fair lady?

He chuckled as he headed for the stables, now *he* was being as fanciful as a girl.

★　★　★

Annabel watched him canter away. He was obviously taking the cross-country route, it would be far quicker to reach the Norwich Road that way. The little lanes around their village meandered and twisted and one could travel miles before you got anywhere at all. Thank goodness he had left, now she could tell Mama what they must do.

She gathered up her skirts and raced downstairs to burst into the parlour. Her mother looked up.

'Good heavens, Annabel. I almost pierced my finger with my needle when you came in like that. Whatever is the matter?'

'We must leave at once, Mama. I know Colonel Sinclair thinks there is time for him to ride to Norwich and back, but he does not know Sir Randolph as we do. Word could have reached him even as we speak. It is barely two days' ride from London, less if he travels post. He could arrive on our doorstep tomorrow morning. He will have constables with him, we would have no recourse but to

167

go back to London under his control. That cannot be allowed to happen.'

She saw her mother's face pale. 'I had not thought of that. You're right, my love. The colonel will be away three nights at the least, and that is too long to be waiting here. Major Dudley would protect us, but at what cost to himself?'

'Then you agree? We must ride to Robert's estate in Hertfordshire. I'm sure Major Dudley will know exactly where it is. We must wait there until the colonel joins us. If we are not at Brandon Hall, then we shall not be discovered immediately.'

Her mother stood. 'We cannot leave until Major Dudley returns. He will understand at once when I have explained the circumstances to him. I did realize, my love, that your marriage would only protect yourself, but that would have been enough for me. Just knowing that you are safe from that monster, shall make me happy. This way, perhaps I can stay out of his clutches as well.'

'I shall go up and pack. You must speak to Mary and then wait until the major returns and persuade him of the urgency. With luck we can be away soon, and have three hours' travelling time before we have to overnight somewhere.'

Leaving her mother to speak to Mary, she

raced back upstairs. She went to her mother's studio first, collected her pallets, paints, pencils, brushes and paper and rammed them in a leather satchel. Mother could not live without these things. Then she hurried to her mother's bedchamber and laid out her riding habit. The royal blue velvet was still like new; her mother had not ridden much since they arrived at Brandon Hall.

In her own chamber she snatched a change of clothes and clean underwear and on impulse added the blue dress from its hook in the closet. She rolled it up and pushed it in the bag as well. She also added the matching slippers. She then stripped and pulled on a clean pair of britches, adding the rest of the man's attire she wore when working in the fields. Boots completed the outfit. She was certain no one would give her a second look. She imagined that when they were seen, her mother and Major Dudley would be taken for a couple and she the groom in attendance.

She slung the leather satchel over her shoulder and took a carpetbag in each hand. She had seen Major Dudley riding across the gravel turning circle. It was time to go.

Her mother was in the entrance hall. 'I have laid out your riding habit, Mama. I have your painting things here. We are ready to leave as soon as Major Dudley has collected his belongings.'

'I have yet to speak to him, my dear. But as we are so pressed for time, I shall leave that task to you. Mary has packed us sufficient food for today and tomorrow. We can collect that as we leave.'

Taking the three bags Annabel headed for the stables hoping to meet the major there. She was in luck, he had barely dismounted when she arrived.

'Major Dudley, we have to leave at once. I cannot tell you how urgent it is.' She thought rapidly, he didn't know that Colonel Sinclair had gone, but neither did he know how close Sir Randolph might be to snatching them back. 'Colonel Sinclair has ridden to get a licence in Norwich, but Mama and I have decided we dare not wait for his return. I shall write a note, telling him that we are going to his estate in Hertfordshire. It was his intention for us to go there, but as the carriage is unavailable he thought we could not do so. We must ride. We need your support in this, Major. Mama is desperate to get away before the monster comes and claims her.'

Her words were enough to convince him. 'If Lady Sophia thinks it's imperative that we leave, then we shall do so. Give me a moment to collect my trappings. I see that you are dressed as a groom. A wise move, Miss Bentley, as a stable boy no one will give you a second glance. I shall leave you to tack up the horses and be back with your mother shortly.'

He hurried away, his face etched with concern. She thought for a moment, then realized she could not possibly ride Silver, it would look decidedly odd if the groom was riding a horse of that calibre. The major must ride her gelding, her mother the hunter, and she would lead one carriage horse and ride the other. She prayed that her mother would be able to control the massive beast.

She tacked up Silver first with no difficulty. However, when she tried to persuade the hunter to accept the side-saddle he viewed it with distaste, and bit and fly kicked until she took it off.

'Botheration! I had better ride you, sir, Mama must take one of the carriage horses. I hope they prove more biddable.'

By the time her mother arrived on the major's arm, he carrying a second leather satchel bulging with food and drink, all four horses were ready.

'Will Mary be able to manage until the new staff arrive?' She turned to the major. 'I assume that new staff are coming soon?'

He nodded. 'Yes, there are three men to take care of the outside duties. They will live in the rooms above the stable, and three women arrive tomorrow morning to help Mrs Hopkins in the house.'

'I have not said a proper farewell to Mary — I could not bear to. She is like a second mother to me. I pray it won't be long before we're all reunited.'

Her mother hurried forward and gathered her into an embrace. 'Don't cry, my darling girl. Major Dudley assures me that once matters are settled, and you are Mrs Sinclair, then the colonel will employ all three of them, if that's how you want to arrange things.'

There was no further conversation, they all knew how urgent the matter was. The baggage was already strapped securely to the riderless horse and it took the major a few moments only to secure the extra satchels.

She watched him tenderly toss her mother into the saddle and push her booted foot into the single stirrup iron. Her eyes widened. Good grief! Is that how things were? She should have realized her mother was becoming interested in the major, she talked of little else when they were alone together. The major vaulted into the saddle leaving her to use the mounting block. He was so preoccupied with taking care of her mama, he appeared to have forgotten she was his responsibility too.

She shrugged, it was better thus. She needed to be treated like a groom, otherwise their disguise would be penetrated immediately. When Sir Randolph arrived and found his quarry flown he would immediately send out search parties. He had the law on his side and could rightfully demand they be returned to him. He would be enquiring for two blonde women riding alone, but no one would see *that* party. A husband and wife, with their groom in attendance, would go unremarked. Her horse was broader than Silver, but not as tall. He had a mouth of iron, but although he had rejected the side-saddle, was perfectly amenable now she was astride.

Mary arrived in the stable yard to wave them off. They could not go across country; she prayed they would not be unfortunate enough to be in the lane at the same time as Rushton. There was only one route leading from Brandon Hall and they could not fail to meet him if he was already in the vicinity.

They had been travelling unremarked for more than an hour when she recalled she had

173

not written a letter to Robert explaining why they had left so precipitously. Mary would have to explain it all to him, it was not ideal, but he would understand why she had left.

13

Sir Randolph glanced at the mantel clock for the third time, how long was it going to be before the damn lawyers deigned to turn up? A second footman had returned more than an hour ago saying they would be with him directly.

He kicked the fire, his boot sending sparks flying out on to the carpet. He ignored them. It was now almost three hours since the note had left the house; it would have been quicker for him to have gone round in person. However, he would not lower himself to visit the insalubrious premises of Gibson and Peabody.

He strode to the window and glared out. Apart from the usual midday traffic, there was no sign of a hackney carriage approaching his front door. A nervous tap drew his attention to the other side of the room. His butler sidled in, carrying what looked suspiciously like a jug of water. What the devil was going on?

'Excuse me, sir, but your carpet appears to be on fire.'

He was suddenly aware of the smell of

burning wool. The expensive carpet in front of the fire was smouldering dangerously, in his preoccupation he had been unaware of it. Furious at his foolishness, he turned his back on his minions and left them to deal with the matter. The sound of water being tipped was followed by clouds of choking smoke.

Incensed his morning had been ruined he stamped out through the dining-room and took the stairs at a run. He kicked his bedchamber door open, shouting for his valet. 'My outer garments at once. Send to the stable. Have my carriage brought round.'

His manservant appeared, Randolph's topcoat in his arms. 'Allow me, Sir Randolph. I have sent the girl down with the message. By the time you are ready, the carriage will be outside.'

'It had better be.'

His valet placed the coat around his shoulders and he pushed his arms through the loose sleeves. Then his man dropped to his knees with a cloth he had extracted from his pocket and quickly polished the boot that had been in the fire. It took a full fifteen minutes before his manservant was satisfied he was ready to face the world.

Randolph was feeling calmer when he left his room. His nostrils filled with the pungent aroma of burning carpet, which had drifted up the central stairwell and immediately his hands clenched. He was not going to remain in the house for a moment longer. His lawyers were due to call at any moment, but he wanted to remove himself from his sniggering staff. He glared at the two footmen who were waiting to open the front door. He didn't need to ask if his carriage was outside, he could hear his driver talking to the groom who was at their heads.

'Where to, Sir Randolph?'

'Drive round the park for half an hour. Then take me to White's.'

He jumped into the vehicle, a footman removed the steps, closing the door behind him. He settled back on the squabs, trying to breathe deeply as his physician had told him. His head hurt and the blood pounded around his body. Doctor Fitzwilliam had warned him it would be the death of him if he didn't learn to curb his temper. He might suffer a fatal apoplexy. That was what the quack had told him, but it was all balderdash. A few deep breaths and a calming ride around the park and he'd be back to normal in no time. He closed his eyes and tried to imagine the waves breaking on a distant shore, golden corn growing in the fields, exactly as that old charlatan told him to. Stuff and nonsense!

What he needed was a large brandy to calm his nerves.

When he returned from his club he was more relaxed, and determined to organize his departure for Suffolk, with or without his lawyers to accompany him.

★ ★ ★

At last! Robert patted the pocket with the licence he had obtained at the bishop's office. It had taken less time than he'd anticipated, but his horse would not be sufficiently rested to begin the long ride back to Brandon Hall.

Norwich was bustling and noisy, it was market day, the streets full of tradespeople, diligences and carts piled high with produce. The pavements were thronged with village and townsfolk eager to buy what was on offer.

He checked his pocket watch, if he left it another three hours, it would be safe to attempt his return journey. If he took it steadily, he ought to complete the ride today. He would fill his time by finding a goldsmith's and purchasing an engagement ring. His mouth curved, no, he had better buy a wedding ring as well.

Two hours later, his purchases alongside the licence, he returned to the inn where he had stayed the night. His mount was a strong beast and should be ready to ride the thirty miles back to Brandon. He had already paid his shot, his bag was being watched over by an ostler, he had only to saddle up and be away.

He clattered out of the cobbled yard determined to complete his journey even if it meant rousing the household in order to get inside. The weather was set fair, the sun surprisingly warm for the start of October.

This time he knew his route, did not have to stop and ask directions as he had done the previous day. He smiled as he cantered along the grass verge. He had accomplished his goal and would only have been away from home two nights. With luck the new staff should be settled in, the house running more smoothly, the larder replenished and the wine cellar full. In two days he would be a married man. When he had left London he had been expecting an uneventful visit to the country, how wrong he had been. For the first time in years he felt happy. He had a beautiful betrothed and a reason to hope his future would not be as bleak as the past.

Keeping his word to Lady Sophia was going to be the most difficult part of the enterprise. He desired Annabel, wanted to make love to her. After living like a monk these past few years it was going to be dammed hard keeping out of her bed.

His fingers tightened involuntarily jerking the reins, his horse stumbled almost unseating him. He cursed volubly at his stupidity. It was time to concentrate on the matter in hand. Brandon Hall was his goal, and making sure Annabel and Lady Sophia were safe. He had a bad feeling about Sir Randolph, feared that he might have arrived in his absence. Major Dudley was as ruthless as he when it came to a fight, but if the legal crows were there, and possibly constables as well, he would have no option but to let them go.

He resisted the urge to kick on, knowing his horse would be blown long before he reached home if he did so. He trotted into the stable yard around nine o'clock. It was black, but there were two lanterns hanging from the wall. He dismounted, tossing his bag to one side and shouting for a groom.

There was the sound of feet coming from the tack room and a man, about his own age, appeared. 'Good evening, your honour. I'm Jim, you must be the colonel.'

'I am, Jim. I have walked my horse the last two miles, so he's cool. Give him extra rations, he's worked hard today.'

'Yes, sir. I can tell you, I'm right glad to have you back, with only the pony to take care of, I've been twiddling my thumbs these past two days.'

God's teeth! No wonder it was quiet, the yard was empty, all the horses gone. 'Where are the horses? Have they been turned out?'

'No, sir, Lady Sophia, Major Dudley and Miss Bentley left here yesterday. No, that ain't right, it must have been the day before. Mrs Hopkins says they left before we arrived.'

Robert was stunned. His brain refused to function. He had anticipated the ladies being snatched back, but not that they would run away from him. He turned away, covering his shock by retrieving his bag from the ground. 'Make sure the horse's well rested, I shall be leaving, myself, tomorrow.'

He walked back to the house not sure what to make of the news. He should be relieved that he no longer had to marry, break his vow to Maria. Instead he felt betrayed, as if his lover had abandoned him, not a girl he scarcely knew.

★   ★   ★

Annabel was finding it far harder than she had anticipated to ride, and lead a horse, at the same time. It was something she had not done before; they had been travelling less than an hour and her arm felt as if it was

181

being dragged from its socket. Her mother was managing perfectly well on her mount, deep in conversation with the major most of the time, ignoring their supposed groom. It was all very well remaining in character, but she was feeling decidedly put out.

In order to maintain the pretence she was going to have to sleep in the stables, eat what she was given, and hope nobody discovered she wasn't what she appeared to be. Not a prospect she was looking forward to. Surely they were going to find somewhere to stop soon?

She kicked the hunter into a canter and thundered up behind the other two horses. Alarmed by the sound of her approach both animals shied, Major Dudley remained firm in the saddle but her mother was unseated. Annabel watched in horror as she tumbled headfirst on to the road. Major Dudley was beside her mother in seconds, whilst she struggled to maintain control of her two horses.

'Major Dudley, how is my mother? That was my fault, I should have remembered she is not an experienced horse-woman.'

He looked up, his expression grim. 'She's conscious, but I fear she has broken her arm.'

'It was not your fault, my love, it was my stupidity. I was not concentrating, I was too busy talking to pay heed. The major is correct, I fear I have broken my left arm. But I am perfectly well apart from that.'

Annabel stood in her stirrups. She could see the countryside around them was deserted, no sign of a house to go to for assistance, no sign of a dwelling of any sort. It was dusk already, in an hour it would be full dark. What were they going to do now that Mama was injured?

Confident her horses were calm she dismounted and tethered them to a convenient branch at the side of the road. Her mother's horse was grazing a hundred yards ahead, Silver trotted up to greet her.

'Good boy, I have missed you too. I'm proud of the way you are behaving without me on board.' She had not mentioned to Major Dudley that Silver rarely went well with anyone other than herself. Scrambling back she approached the loose animal. It made no objection to her leaning down and taking the reins. She returned and dismounted, looping the reins over her arm.

'Mama, I am so sorry. What can I do to help?'

'Remain with the horses, Miss Bentley. I shall take care of Lady Sophia.' The major's voice was stern, even if Mama didn't blame her, he did. She watched as he tenderly assisted her mother to her feet. He had removed his stock and fashioned a sling from it, in which the damaged arm was cradled.

'Don't look so worried, my darling girl. I am perfectly well, it hardly hurts at all. I believe that I can ride if Major Dudley leads my horse.'

'Major Dudley, I can see nothing ahead of us, I am concerned there is no sign of habitation.'

'The matter is in hand, Miss Bentley. When we passed through the last hamlet, you might remember I spoke to one of the inhabitants. He told me there is a crossroads ahead. If we turn left and travel for a mile we shall find a decent coaching inn, The King's Head. Even as things are, I'm certain we shall make it before it's too dark to see.'

She prayed he was correct. Her mother didn't seem to need her help, allowing the major to fuss around, and then lift her bodily into the saddle. She was able to clutch the pommel with her sound hand, and hopefully that would be enough to keep her secure, if they travelled slowly.

Should she ask for a leg up? There was nothing suitable to use as a mounting block. She turned, deciding she would have to lengthen a stirrup leather and try to mount that way.

'Allow me, my dear. I'm sorry if I seem a little brusque, but your mother is in a great deal of pain. I'm concerned for her. It is imperative we find shelter and a physician as soon as possible.' He grasped her leg and tossed her into the saddle. 'She's being very stoic at the moment. However, the jolting once we start could cause her to swoon.'

'I understand. You must do everything you can for her. We are both most grateful for your help.'

'You are doing magnificently, my dear. No one could ask for more. The accident was not of your doing, it was my fault.'

He remounted Silver and they moved off, he leading Mama, she behind. The blame lay with them all equally, according to the major, which made her feel less guilty. She wasn't sure if she was glad her mother had found someone to take care of her after being so long on her own. She could only see the growing attachment between them ending in inevitable heartache.

★   ★   ★

Robert tried the side door and, as he'd expected, it had been left unlocked. He was unhappy to be creeping in unannounced, as if he was a burglar. Still, he had no need to tell

185

the staff he was there. He went upstairs to the chamber he'd used previously, the lantern he'd taken from the stable, in his hand. His bed had been stripped and remade with fresh linen. There was water in the jug and fresh towels waiting on the rail.

Dispirited that his journey had been in vain, he tossed his clothes on to a nearby chair and fell into bed in his undergarments. He would wash in the morning, he was too damned tired tonight.

The sound of curtains being drawn back roused him and he pushed himself on to one elbow to see a strange girl smiling shyly at him.

'Mrs Hopkins says as I was to bring you a tray, so, as I ain't sure what you likes, sir, you got a bit of everything.'

He smiled. Obviously the indoor staff were as short of work as the groom. He had never been brought his breakfast on a tray before, apart from the one occasion he had been struck down by the influenza when a boy at school.

'Whatever it is, I'm sure it will be excellent. Tell Hopkins I shall be down to see her directly.' He paused, this wasn't the time to ask about Annabel's disappearance, but the girl should know how Tom and Fred were doing. 'How are Tom Hopkins and Fred?

What did the doctor say, do you happen to know?'

The girl approached the bed, a broad grin making her plain face, pretty. 'Yes, sir, I do that. Mr Tom is still poorly, but he's awake, and taking gruel. Fred would be up and doing already if his ma would let him. The doctor says they're both to stay put until he comes again tomorrow.'

The girl had left the tray tantalizingly out of reach. Robert wasn't sure if he should step out of bed, dressed as he was, to collect it or wait until the girl had gone. He was damned hungry; he hadn't stopped to eat yesterday and the smell of newly baked bread and coffee was making his mouth water.

The girl hovered uncertainly in the centre of the room, obviously not sure what her duties were. He would make it easy for her. 'That will be all.'

She bobbed a curtsy and vanished into the dressing-room and he could hear her clattering down the back stairs to the kitchen. No sooner had she gone than he was out of bed and across to the food. He devoured everything with relish. His stomach full, he felt more sanguine about matters. He had done his best to help Annabel, but she had chosen to reject him. Dudley was responsible for them now, he had fulfilled his duty, kept

187

his promise, it was done. He would wash and shave, speak to Hopkins, make sure they had sufficient funds to be going on with and then . . . he shrugged, then he could do what he pleased. Why did the prospect fill him with despair?

An hour later he walked into the kitchen the empty tray in his hand. Another girl from the village and the housekeeper were busy about their duties.

'Lawks a mercy! You shouldn't have brought that down, sir, the girl would have fetched it.'

'Well, it's here now, Hopkins. I'm glad to hear that both patients are making good progress. I should like to talk to you, could you join me in the small parlour?'

He left her to wipe her floury hands on her apron and could hear her bustling along behind him. He waited by the unlit fire. 'Sit down, please, I have no wish to stand on ceremony.' He waited for her to do so; she was obviously uncomfortable sitting in his presence. With a sigh he straddled a chair and faced her. 'Can you tell me anything about the departure of Lady Sophia, Miss Bentley, and Major Dudley?'

'No, sir, apart from they left in a hurry like. They didn't say why they were leaving so sharpish or where they were going. I'm as

188

puzzled as you, sir, that they didn't wait. I packed some food and they set off. Did Miss Bentley not leave you a note?'

He shook his head. 'No, not that I've found, and I've looked everywhere. I shall leave you with sufficient funds to be going on with, but I must return to Town immediately.'

'Of course you must go, Colonel. Miss Bentley is your responsibility, you must find her wherever she is.'

His jaw tightened, how dare she presume to give him instructions? He was about to reprimand her when he belatedly understood that far from being a free agent, his life had just become more complicated. Until Annabel told him in person that the arrangement was cancelled it must stand. The housekeeper was staring at him anxiously.

'Are you unwell, sir? You've gone right poorly looking.'

'Thank you, Hopkins, but I am quite recovered. Forgive me, did the vicar visit in my absence?'

'He did, sir, and the funeral for poor Jethro is to be held tomorrow morning. I took the liberty of giving all the staff the morning off to attend, I hope that's acceptable?'

'Excellent, you've done well. Did Major Dudley or Lady Sophia have the opportunity to speak to the vicar?'

'No, sir, and not to the doctor, neither. They had been gone several hours before they arrived.'

'Very well. You may return to your duties.'

He was left to his thoughts, and they weren't happy ones. Annabel had decided she would rather go off penniless than tie herself to him. He didn't blame her; he was irascible and autocratic, not a fit partner for anyone. If she knew what had happened in Spain she'd want no more of him.

Where the hell was Dudley taking them? He slammed his hand on to a side table and it collapsed. Dudley had a small estate somewhere to the south of London. That was where he would find them. He stared down at the debris around his feet and wondered whether to clear it or leave it to one of the new maids.

Suddenly the door burst open and Mary stood there her face pale. 'Colonel, he's come. Sir Randolph is here and he's brought the constables and other folk with him.'

14

Annabel followed, fearing her mother might tumble again and make her injury worse. It took them an hour to cover that last mile or so, Major Dudley kept the horses at a slow walk to make sure nothing untoward could happen a second time.

Eventually he turned in his saddle. 'Can you see, Miss Bentley, this is a main thoroughfare, the inn must be that large building half a mile away.'

'I can see it, sir. You do realize that I must remain outside? If my disguise is to remain unpenetrated, I must be given no special treatment. I'm your groom, not Lady Sophia's daughter.'

'We have discussed that, my dear. If you insist on sleeping with Silver then I'm sure you will be safe. It would be a brave man indeed who came near you under those circumstances.'

She shook her head, why should anyone wish to come near a stable boy? She nodded. Of course, they could believe she had rich pickings about her person, people were murdered for far less in the backstreets of London,

191

'Do you intend to register as a married couple?'

'We do; that way I can keep Lady Sophia safe. It is unfortunate, but her safety comes before her reputation on this occasion.'

Reassured by this, her shoulders began to unknot. She didn't care if she had to sleep in the hay, as long as she could sleep. Major Dudley shouted for assistance as soon as they entered the yard. Immediately two ostlers rushed out from the stable block, and the landlord appeared at the front door.

'My good man, my wife has taken a tumble and broken her arm. We require two of your best rooms, and the name of a physician.' He glanced dismissively in her direction. 'Young Sam will take care of my horse, your ostlers must take care of the others.' Major Dudley removed his riding cape and tossed it in her direction. 'Sam, give this a thorough clean by tomorrow.'

The landlord obviously recognized the voice of authority and did not quibble. Her mother, leaning heavily on the major's arm, walked unsteadily towards the entrance, leaving Annabel to continue the charade. One of the grooms turned to her.

'Here, boy, you take this evil beast, he's tried to take a lump out of me already.'

Keeping her head down, she answered

gruffly, 'He's a right terror, that one. I'm the only one what can look after him, apart from the master. You give him here.' Silver's reins were tossed in her direction and instantly the snapping and rearing ceased.

'Blooming marvellous! Look at that, he's only a lad, and that horse's happy to go with him quiet as a lamb.'

The stables were well equipped, the individual stalls knee deep in clean straw, the manger full of hay and a fresh bucket of water waiting by the door. She removed Silver's tack and hung it on the wooden pegs high on the wall, out of the reach of inquisitive equine noses.

'There you are, Silver. I shall find you some oats, and see if there's anything for me at the kitchen door.' No, she didn't need to go to the kitchen and risk being exposed for what she was not, there was still ample food in the saddle-bags that had been slung across the pack horse.

'I'm to take the master and mistress's bags to them, but the saddle-bags are to stay with me. I'm sleeping with the master's horse. He'll not settle otherwise.'

'Suit yourself, lad. There's plenty of room upstairs with us, if you want.' The man handed over the bags.

'Is there any hard feed for the horses?

They'll go all the better tomorrow if there is.'

'In the fodder bin at the end, help yourself. All part of the price.'

She was left surrounded by baggage, the two men went to fetch the necessary food for the three animals they were taking care of. Taking the two leather satchels into Silver's stall, she buried them in a corner. Then with the three carpet-bags she headed to the rear of the inn. She knew better than to barge into the kitchen, so hovered outside looking suitably humble.

'Excuse me, ma'am, I have the bags for my master and mistress.'

A plump woman, with flour-streaked cheeks, appeared at the door. 'You're not coming in with that muck on your boots, young man. Give them here, my Jesse will take them.' A small girl, not more than ten years old, stepped out moments later.

'Here, boy, I'm to take the bags. You get yourself back to the stable where you belong.'

Hiding her smile, Annabel handed them over keeping her head lowered. She was a good six inches taller than the child, but had been put firmly in her place. In the world of servants, outside was definitely inferior to being employed in the house.

Whilst sitting on the floor of the loose box she heard the ostlers' conversation without being seen herself. One of them was to go and fetch the doctor, and he wasn't best pleased about it. Satisfied everything was being done for her mother, she unbuckled the saddle-bags, drank the lemonade from the flagon, and curled up under the major's riding coat for the night.

Major Dudley appeared bright and early next morning. However, she had already been up an hour or more, seen to the horses, and been delighted to find that the substantial breakfast brought round by the small girl was also part of the deal. By now her face was so grimy, she was sure not even her best friend would recognize her.

'Miss Bentley, my dear, I can give you news of your mother. Lady Sophia has been visited by the physician who has set her arm. It is a bad fracture, and the swelling and bruising far worse than it would have been if we had not had to ride on after the accident.'

'Is she well in herself?'

'Yes, my dear. She's remarkably cheerful considering the circumstances. She said to tell you that we have registered as Major and Mrs Dudley. The doctor is adamant that we must not leave for several days, a putrid infection could set in at the break if we do not abide by his instructions.'

'Several days? This is a disaster. Sir

Randolph will surely discover us by then. When he arrives at Brandon Hall and finds us gone, he will immediately employ search parties. It won't take long for him to learn that we are here.'

He patted her shoulder. 'You must not worry, my dear girl. Let me take care of things for you. Whatever happens, Lady Sophia insists you're to remain hidden out here.' He rummaged in his pocket and produced a small leather bag. 'Here, take this. If you have to, there's enough money for you to get away safely. You must go at once to Sinclair's estate in Hertfordshire. You remember the directions I gave you yesterday?'

She nodded miserably. 'Yes, I do. I shall not want to leave Mama behind, but I'll do as she asks.'

'Good girl. Are they treating you well out here? How did you manage . . . well, manage things in order to keep your true identity secret?'

She grinned in spite of her worries. 'I used the facilities in the middle of the night. My cap is voluminous, and I have so much hair plaited under it, it would not shift in a hurricane.'

He chuckled. 'Take care of yourself, my dear, I promise you no harm shall come to your mama.'

So that was how it was. She could hardly credit that two adults of mature years had fallen in love so precipitously. She sighed, if only Robert felt the same for her, she might believe everything would turn out for the best.

★ ★ ★

Robert was aghast. 'How can you be sure this is Lady Sophia's husband, Hopkins?'

'There are *two* carriages, and who else could it be? They just turned into the drive, as you know it's in a parlous state, so they'll need to take their time getting here. I reckon we've got around ten minutes before they arrive.'

'Excellent. You must inform them that Lady Sophia and Miss Bentley have gone to visit Major Dudley's sister at Brandon Manor. That should send them on a wild goose chase and delay things for half a day at least. I shall leave immediately to find them.'

The woman didn't argue, no one did when he gave commands. He smiled, apart from Annabel, that is. His bag was already packed, all he had to do was collect it. He left by the side door and ran to the stables his sword clanking at his side, his pistols heavy in his pockets. The groom had already saddled his horse. There was one thing more he needed to add before he left, his rifle, which was wrapped in oil cloth in the carriage he had arrived in.

'Good man, remember, say nothing about my being here. And Lady Sophia and Miss Bentley have gone to Brandon Manor for a short visit. Make sure the other men say the same.'

'Yes, sir, got that clear.'

Five minutes later Robert vaulted into the saddle, having secured everything behind him, and cantered off down the track that led away from the main drive. He was a mile away in minutes and certain he was undiscovered.

Now, which way would they have gone? They would have to head for London, and travel by back roads, not the main thorough-fares. After several false starts, and roundabout routes, he came across a hamlet in which a local resident remembered seeing them pass through. He was only twenty minutes, it would appear, from a main thoroughfare, but still two days behind them. He must have covered the same distance as them in a fraction of the time, but it would still be another day before he would catch up.

He turned left at the crossroads and spotted a coaching inn ahead of him. It was possible they had called in there for refreshments, he would stop and make enquiries. He could do with a drink, and his horse would benefit from a rub down and an hour's rest. He reduced his pace, not wanting to arrive pell-mell and arouse suspicion. He trotted into the yard; the first person he saw was a scruffy stable lad looking suspiciously like his missing betrothed.

★   ★   ★

Randolph could hardly contain his excitement. Another mile and he would have done it. He had made sure he got the legal matters straight before he left, and had brought a maid to attend the ladies. He had got his man of affairs, Hughes, to bring along a couple of his henchmen dressed as if they were constables. The four of them should have no difficulty manhandling Sophia and Annabel into the carriage when the time came to leave.

'You know what you have to do, Hughes?'

The man was sprawled untidily in the corner of the coach, his narrow face and sallow complexion making him look consumptive. This was deceptive, the man was tough and skilled, not only in matters of finance, but also in the less salubrious dealings he was occasionally instructed to handle.

'Yes, Sir Randolph; I'm to remain behind you, and if there is any resistance, to restrain Lady Sophia, leaving Miss Bentley to yourself.'

Randolph shifted on the seat, he couldn't wait to have Annabel struggling in his arms. The carriage stopped. He flung the door open and jumped out. With his black topcoat swirling around him, his beaver low over his eyes, he strode towards the front door knowing he made a fearsome sight. He was reckoned a tall man, and well set up, and until ladies knew different, they believed he was as charming as he was handsome.

He hammered on the front door not really expecting it to be opened. The two men who had scrambled out of the second coach could effect an entry if they were locked out. He heard the clatter of feet approaching and the door opened. A woman of middle years, her faded brown hair pushed tidily under a cap, apron pristine, curtsied politely.

'I beg your pardon, my lord, but there's nobody in residence at present.'

'Get out of my way, you wretched woman.' He pushed past her, determined to see for himself whether she was lying. He looked round, the house was in good order, the appointments not luxurious, but adequate. He gestured to Hughes. 'Get your men to search this place from top to bottom. If they are here, find them and bring them to me.'

'Excuse me, my lord, but Lady Sophia and Miss Bentley have gone to visit Lady Barton at Brandon Manor, it's no more than ten miles from here. I'm not expecting them back until the end of next week.'

'When did they leave?'

The woman paled, her smile slipping. 'Two days ago, sir. Her ladyship didn't say as they were expecting any visitors. I could send one of the grooms with you, they would show you the route, if that would be of any assistance?'

Randolph finally accepted he had been thwarted yet again. Who the devil was Lady Barton and why should Sophia be visiting her? He would rest here for an hour or so, then get the groom to give them directions to this Brandon Manor.

'I shall require refreshments to be served at once. My horses need watering and I have several members of staff who require feeding.'

The woman curtsied nervously. 'Of course, sir, I shall have my girls lay up in the small parlour for your staff, and in the dining-room for yourself. If you would care to wait in the drawing-room, I'll have coffee sent right away.'

'Coffee? Dammit, woman, I want brandy.'

'Yes sir, it will be with you directly.'

He glanced up and saw two maids hovering in the background. One went to the double doors at the far side of the vestibule and pulled them apart. She didn't speak, just curtsied and then scurried away after the older woman.

When he returned to his carriage he was feeling more sanguine about the outcome of this second journey. The route to Brandon Manor was straightforward, they should arrive during the afternoon, and the more he considered this fresh turn of events the better he liked it. It would be far easier to reclaim his wife and daughter if they were in public: no woman would wish to make a scene with others watching.

★ ★ ★

Annabel dropped the bucket of water she was carrying, soaking her britches and filling her boot. 'Colonel Sinclair, I had not expected to see you. Look what you've made me do! I am drenched to the bone.'

'Good God! What are you doing here? I thought you would be almost in London by now.'

She noticed one of the ostlers had stopped

202

to gawp. She couldn't talk to him here, they must have privacy. 'The master will be right pleased to see you, sir. A real bit of luck it is, you passing by like this. Mrs Dudley's gone and broke her arm, sir, and can't move for a day or two longer. I'll show you where to put your horse, sir, if you care to follow me.'

The ostler moved away, accepting what he saw, as a fortuitous encounter with a family friend. As soon as they were private she turned to him, her face anxious. 'Why are you here? How did you find us? I'm so sorry, I forgot to leave you a note explaining that we were going directly to your estate in Hertfordshire. Four days was too long, Sir Randolph would have found us before you returned.'

'My estate? I should have thought of that. How badly injured is your mother? Rushton is already at Brandon Hall. I arranged to have him sent on a wild goose chase to Brandon Manor. But I should think, by this evening, he will have discovered this deception and be baying for your blood.'

'I feared as much, in fact I expected him sooner. We cannot leave here for at least another forty-eight hours, Mama's arm is still so swollen it would be dangerous for her to move.'

'I have an idea. You and your mother could be taken for siblings. You must get inside and put on her riding habit. Dudley must pay his shot — pretend they're leaving. I shall book *their* room, and later Major Dudley and I shall change places, and you and your mother shall do the same.'

'But you look nothing like Major Dudley, how can this deception work?'

He grinned, his teeth a flash of white in the gloom. 'Your stepfather knows neither Dudley nor me. If we travel together as Major and Mrs Dudley, why should he think we are not who we appear to be?'

She frowned. 'But we have no groom to accompany us, someone to lead the baggage horse.'

'I shall take the landlord and his good lady into our confidence, spin him some story about disgruntled suitors — not the truth of course. If I give him enough money I'm certain he will be only too happy to fall in with our plans and supply us with a groom.'

'Hire a boy from here? That would be perfect. Major Dudley and Mama can remain . . . ' There was something about this scheme that didn't quite fit. 'I do not understand how Colonel Sinclair can suddenly have acquired a wife when he arrived here on his own.'

'Lady Sophia shall remain invisible, of course, until the danger is passed.'

'But they will be obliged to share one bedchamber.'

He nodded. 'I rather think it's too late to worry about propriety. When your mother chose to travel as Major Dudley's wife she would have known her reputation was in tatters.'

He was right. There was no time to stand chattering, she had to work out a way of getting inside without being seen and then disguising herself as her mother.

15

Robert finished explaining his scheme to Lady Sophia. 'Annabel must somehow be brought up here; we do not wish the other guests to see her; they will not be so reticent when my husband starts blustering and bullying.'

'There are back stairs. Whilst the luncheon rush is on, and all the staff are fully occupied, she can creep in then. The landlord and his wife are only too happy to help, especially as I have given them five guineas for their trouble.'

Her eyebrows flickered. Such largesse did not often come her way, now it was being tossed to strangers on her behalf. Whatever happened, he would make it his business neither Annabel nor her mother ever had to suffer penury again. He had nothing to spend his money on but himself and it would give him the greatest pleasure to help them.

'I have bespoken this room, and this parlour and as soon as your daughter is ready I shall leave you and the major here.'

Major Dudley coloured. 'I shall sleep in here, that goes without saying, Sinclair.'

Lady Sophia's laugh filled the room

lightening the atmosphere. 'My dear Major Dudley, I believe it is rather late to worry about protecting my reputation. If you sleep out here it will give rise to comment when the chambermaid comes. Why should you be sleeping in here when there is a perfectly good bed in your bedchamber?'

Robert could see his friend was still hesitating. 'Lady Sophia is right, Dudley, as far as the rest of the staff, and the guests are concerned, you will be Colonel Sinclair and staying here alone.'

'The staff have seen the major, surely they will mention that it is he who is here, and not someone called Colonel Sinclair?'

He grinned. 'I have thought of that as well, my lady. I shall be stricken down with a highly infectious fever. Only the landlord shall come in to wait on me, other staff will go no further than here. Dudley, go down and pay your bill. I shall follow directly to start complaining about feeling unwell. This will give you time to move your belongings.' All he had to do was feign illness, and the masquerade was started.

He had already primed Annabel. George, the landlord's son, who was to accompany them, was to go round and tell her when the coast was clear. He walked into the dining-room and staggered dramatically, crashing noisily against two tables and making quite certain that every head was turned in his direction.

'I beg your pardon, I felt a trifle unsteady. I shall be all right when I sit down.'

He pulled out a chair and slumped dramatically, resting his head on the table and moaning slightly, muttering about how hot it was and how much his head was aching. It was quite positive he had everybody's full attention. He remained where he was mumbling as if in a delirium, and then on cue, the landlady appeared beside him.

'Colonel Sinclair, sir, I believe you're very unwell. I hope it is not the infectious fever you have brought with you. You will need to remain here a day or so. I have sent for my husband, he shall escort you to a bedchamber. We shall send for the physician immediately.'

He allowed himself to be hoisted upright, bundled out of the dining-room and up the stairs. With suitable moans, groans and staggers he entered the room he had recently vacated. He could hear the sound of Annabel's voice next door.

★ ★ ★

Annabel nodded to the landlord's son, George. 'I must go, the colonel's waiting for

208

me.' The boy Robert had engaged, who was roughly her size and dressed in similar fashion, smiled happily.

'This is a bit of allright, nothing so exciting has ever happened to me, I can tell you. You go along, I shall start tacking up the horses.'

Annabel wondered what his reaction would be if he knew she was a girl. He'd been told she was to act as valet to Sinclair whilst he was unwell. She slipped away round the side of the building until she came to a side entrance, which had been left ajar.

It was deserted; she heard the clatter and rattle of pots and pans coming from the kitchen a little way along a narrow corridor. The tiny stairwell was quiet. Not bothering to take a candle, having been told it was twenty-three steps to the door she required.

With eyes shut, she counted, and then pushed. To her relief a door opened and she was directly outside the chamber she required. The corridor was empty, what guests there were, were downstairs enjoying their luncheon. The other rooms on this corridor were empty, waiting for the next wave of overnight travellers to arrive later in the day.

She dashed across the corridor and into the parlour to find Major Dudley waiting.

'Miss Bentley, we have been expecting you.

209

Your mama is in the bedchamber, she has everything ready.' He viewed her dubiously. 'Although I think it is going to take somewhat longer than we anticipated, you will need to be a deal cleaner before you effect your transformation.'

She laughed. 'Dirt is a good disguise, sir, even the young lad who's taking my place has not recognized that I am female.'

'I have moved all my belongings into the bedchamber which is why it is somewhat cluttered. You had better hurry, it will not be long before the colonel is brought upstairs.'

She entered the room and her mother held out her good arm. 'Darling girl, I have been so worried about you living in the stables. My word, how dirty you are. Never mind, there's plenty of water and it's still reasonably warm. Quickly, remove your garments and get yourself clean.'

'Mama, never mind about me, how are you?'

'My arm will do very well, my dear, it hardly hurts at all. However, if you do not leave these premises in the next hour our efforts to escape might be wasted. Rushton will not remain long at Brandon Manor when he discovers our deception. He might very well be looking for us at this very moment.'

She needed no further urging, in less than

fifteen minutes she was dressed in her mother's riding habit. It fitted as if it had been made for her. She must have filled out recently.

'My darling, you look exactly like me. But without the wrinkles of course.'

'You have no wrinkles, Mama, and well you know it. Do I have the hat at the right angle? If I pull the veil lower it will obscure the top of my face, make it even more difficult for anyone to know it's not Lady Sophia they see. The colonel has even given me a sling for my arm. He's a resourceful man, I'm sure this plan will work and keep us all safe.'

Sinclair, sounding at death's door, was approaching the parlour. It was time for her to leave.

'Mama, I must go now, I don't know when we'll meet again, but I trust Major Dudley to take care of you. Remember, as soon as you can, you must hire a post chaise and remove yourself to Major Dudley's estate.'

'I shall do that, my love. We shall be reunited again very soon. Now, let me look at you.' Her mother stepped back to admire the transformation. 'I don't want you to worry about me. This is all very exciting. I have not had so much fun in years.'

Annabel smiled, that was exactly what the innkeeper's son had said. Was she the only one not enjoying the experience? She was scared witless, convinced that their disguise would be penetrated, that Sir Randolph would arrive and capture them at any moment. She knew their protectors would fight to keep them safe; Robert could be killed. She couldn't bear to think of it.

'Take care of yourself, Mama. I love you and pray that we are together again soon.' She hugged her mother and rushed from the room before she broke down. In the parlour the two men, who had been conversing quietly, stopped in mid sentence. Major Dudley was the first to recover.

'Miss Bentley, if I did not know, I would have thought you Lady Sophia. I have sent the bags down and asked for the horses to be brought round. Now, all I have to do is escort you outside.'

The colonel finally found his voice. 'I shall leave now, although I will be on foot, I should be waiting by the time you arrive. I shall sprint a half-mile down the road and wait in the coppice on the left. We shall be sufficiently distant from here to be unobserved.'

He had thought of everything. She had a dreadful feeling it might be a long time before she saw her mother again. She had expected to be heartbroken, but for some unaccountable reason she found herself excited at the prospect of travelling alone with Robert.

Gathering up the skirt of her riding habit, she hooked it over her arm and was ready to begin the deception, it was possible there were guests wandering around. She heard the door click. The colonel had already crept off and would be away across the fields. She left the parlour, Major Dudley fussing at her side. The landlord appeared in the vestibule to bid them farewell, which he did more effusively than was customary.

'I bid you farewell, Major Dudley, madam. I hope that your arm's fully recovered soon. I have sent ahead to make a reservation for you at the White Horse, you should reach it easily by late afternoon.' He bowed, she nodded and Major Dudley smiled politely.

Outside the horses were stamping, impatient to be off after having been cooped up in the stables for so long. Silver was jumping out of his skin, she hoped the major was up to riding him when the horse was so excitable. He lifted her into the saddle, helping her arrange herself.

'If you're ready, my dear, let us depart. We cannot travel fast, and I wish to be at the White Horse in good time.'

It had been decided she and the colonel should head for Norwich as the landlord and his wife had no idea from which direction they had come originally. By doing this, it would give her mother and Dudley time to put distance between themselves and pursuit, as they would be travelling towards London not away from it.

This road ran directly to the market-town and it was to be hoped that they would arrive there before Sir Randolph overtook them. It would be far harder to locate them once they were hidden away in a small hotel.

Riding side-saddle again was a strange sensation but she soon fell into the rhythm, the horse had a long easy stride and was far lighter in the mouth than the hunter she had ridden previously. They had not been travelling far when she saw the coppice. Soon she would have to say goodbye to the major, and her last link with her mama would be gone.

She guided the horse into the trees and he followed. Robert was waiting, scarcely out of breath. 'Excellent, you have made good time. Hurry up, Dudley, let's get this over with.'

Why did he sound so impatient? Was there more danger than she understood? Minutes later they were back on the road, Major Dudley left behind, and were heading towards Norwich. She had no wish to make conversation, her heart was too full, so she kept her head lowered.

After fifteen minutes she took a few surreptitious glances at her companion; it did nothing to reassure her. His expression was grave, his eyes constantly moving from side to side, and she realized he was wearing a sword, and had a rifle attached to the rear of the saddle. She was horrified by the thought of the violence that might be involved before this episode came to a satisfactory conclusion.

If anything happened to Robert she would be distraught. Her fingers jerked the reins causing her mount to toss its head and stumble. She was being as cautious as Mama. In spite of her reservations about his character she now found herself in love with her companion. Her spirits lifted. The outlook seemed less bleak — could he possibly feel the same for her? His face was unsmiling; either he was concerned about this escapade or disliked his companion.

She had already removed her arm from the sling, pushing the unwanted piece of material into her pocket. She had to get away from him, ride alone until she had regained control of her troublesome thoughts. She clicked to her horse digging her heel into its side. Immediately they were cantering along the grass verge and her companion was obliged to follow.

Suddenly Robert's hand reached across and pulled her horse to a halt. 'What the devil do you think you're playing at? Do you want another accident on your conscience?'

It was only then she remembered poor George. She twisted round and saw that he had parted company with the hunter and released his hold on the baggage horse. 'I did not think. You must go back at once and see if he's injured.' This was her second error.

'Do not presume to give me orders, young lady. Remain here. If you move an inch you will regret it.'

Why was he so rude to her? She had not meant to cause the accident, and George was already on his feet and scrambling back into the saddle. She braced herself for a further set down.

'If you attempt anything so foolhardy as cantering a second time, Miss Bentley, I shall put on a leading rein.'

'You are impossible, sir. I have already apologized. I had forgotten about George. I'm hardly likely to do so again, I'm not an imbecile.' For an awful moment she thought she had gone too far, his eyes narrowed and she saw his hand clench. Was he going to strike her? Was that the kind of man she had agreed to marry, had inexplicably fallen in love with?

She turned her head away in despair. She must not make the same mistake her mother had, and marry a violent man. He might be as brutal as the one they were fleeing from. Her inattention caused her mount to peck; this would not do. Lack of concentration would cause another accident.

The further they travelled without being intercepted the greater her belief that all would be well. She must forget about her own problems, as long as her mother did not have to go back to her husband she would be content. By the time Sir Randolph caught up with them it would be too late for her stepfather to snatch back his errant wife. She would be safe at the major's estate.

She forced herself to take an interest in her surroundings, enjoy the autumn sunshine on her face, the feel of a good horse beneath her. Robert had taken the lead rein of the baggage horse which meant they could increase their speed. This time she was able to canter without being roared at. They had been walking for an hour when he came over to her.

'We can rest here for a while, there's a stream the horses can drink from and we have a picnic the landlady provided.'

Obediently she reined back. Not waiting for him to dismount and help her, she kicked her foot free and dropped to the ground. Leading her horse to the water she let it step in to drink. She was still confused about her feelings. How could she love a man she feared? There was no question of marrying him the way she felt at the moment.

He appeared unaware of her reserve and treated her with his usual impersonal charm. When she had failed to respond for the third time he came over to her. 'What's wrong? Are you still cross with me for shouting at you? I apologize, you must learn that it means nothing. I still have barrack-room manners.'

Her fears seemed absurd in the face of his apology. 'I am not used to being bullied, sir, but I accept your apology.'

'Bullied? God's teeth! Is that how it appears to you? Do you consider me in the same light as Rushton?'

Her face paled. She could not answer. He came closer, reaching out to brush her cheek lightly with his fingers sending an unexpected shiver down her spine.

'Sweetheart, what a brute I have been. I promise I shall do better. From this point onwards I shall be the epitome of politeness and not a cross word shall pass my lips.'

She giggled. 'Now you are being nonsensical. Kindly remove yourself and let me prepare our luncheon.'

He didn't move. 'Come now, if I am to stop bullying you, you must promise to stop giving me orders as if I was your lackey.'

'I promise. Indeed, sir, if we both are able to keep these vows our friends will no longer recognize us.'

His rich chuckle sent further tremors down her spine. She stepped around him and saw that George had already laid out the picnic. The boy grinned at her.

'It's all ready, Mrs Dudley, if you and the major would like to come and eat.'

Good grief! How could they have been so slack that it had taken a servant to remind them of who they were supposed to be? From this point forward she must address the colonel as Dudley and he speak to her as if she was his wife.

They were travelling as a couple — would they be obliged to share the same bedchamber? Her heart skipped a beat. Surely not? The landlord would have reserved two chambers, after all he knew how matters stood between them. No, this was an unnecessary concern. She was certain that when he had seen her as a filthy stable boy all his desire would have evaporated. He would have no interest in her in *that* way, had only offered to keep her safe. He would not pre-empt their wedding night, or wish to do so. In fact the more she considered the matter the safer she felt in his company.

From now on she would try and regard him as an uncle, and not as a prospective bridegroom. This would make matters easier between them. He must not discover she had come to love him — she would remain aloof. However, she would not agree to marry him unless he declared his love for her.

★ ★ ★

Robert's breath hissed through his teeth. He cursed his clumsiness. His preoccupation with keeping her safe had made him forget why they were fleeing in the first place. He felt the all-too-familiar tightening in his groin; she had been enchanting dressed as a stable boy, but in the riding habit she was unbelievably desirable.

An image of his first beloved's ravaged face engulfed him. He forced his mind away from the shocking memory. He must concentrate on the present. Whatever his doubts of his suitability he had given his word.

Annabel was unsure about the proposed marriage, and he had done nothing to reassure her by his behaviour. Surely she must realize it was imperative they be married before they reached Norwich? He had deliberately selected The White Horse as their resting place because the landlord had informed him the vicarage was next door.

Before the day was over she would be his wife; whatever her reservations, she had no choice. He could not protect her unless he was her husband. He just hoped he could convince her of that when the time came to say their vows.

He didn't think he could truly love another woman, but he would be a faithful husband and loving father to any children they might have.

16

Sir Randolph clutched the strap as the carriage swayed between two imposing gate posts. 'We are here at last, it was a deal further than we were led to believe. It will be dark very shortly, this Lady Barton will have to put us up for the night.'

Hughes straightened. 'It's a grand house, sir, there are plenty of rooms. Lady Sophia will be surprised to see us arriving on her doorstep, and her daughter also. I was wondering, this Major Dudley who has accompanied her, do you think he's her fancy man?'

Randolph's fist clenched, his arm shot out, knocking Hughes from the seat. 'How dare you speak in that way. Remember your place.'

The man remained crouched on the floor for a few moments, sniffing loudly, before scrambling back to the seat. His eye was already closing where the fist had made contact.

'I beg your pardon, Sir Randolph, I meant no harm.'

Further conversation was impossible as the coach halted. He waited for the groom to scramble down from the box, open the door and let the steps down. By the time this had been effected the front door of the enormous manor house was open, candlelight flooding on to the marble steps. The butler, an elderly man, walked stiffly towards them, flanked by two bewigged footmen.

Randolph waited for him on the gravel turning circle. 'I am Sir Randolph Rushton, I have come from London to see Lady Barton. She is not expecting me, but I am hoping that she can offer us overnight accommodation.'

'You are most welcome, Sir Randolph, how many chambers shall you require?'

The butler had obviously seen the second coach trundling up behind them. 'One for myself, and somewhere for my man of business. There are also several members of my staff who require accommodation, I care not where you put *them*.' He gestured to the rear of his own carriage. 'My trunk is there, one of my men can bring it in for me.'

He followed his guide into a spacious entrance hall, there was no evidence of the lady of the house, in fact no evidence of anyone apart from servants. A tall, thin woman, dressed in navy bombazine, curtsied as he approached.

'I am Watson, housekeeper here at your service. If you would care to follow me, sir, I will show you to your apartment. Lady Barton's dining out tonight; she will be returning first thing in the morning. I'm sure she will wish you to make yourself welcome until then.'

God dammit! 'And her guests, do they stay overnight with her as well?'

The housekeeper paused and nodded. 'Yes they have all gone to dine; it's too far to drive back so they are staying. They will be back by noon tomorrow.'

There was nothing he could do about it, fate was conspiring against him. But at least he knew he had come to the right place. All he had to do was make himself comfortable, and be ready to pounce when his unsuspecting wife and daughter appeared the next day.

* * *

Annabel saw a sign reading The White Horse swinging in the breeze a hundred yards ahead of them. It was scarcely mid-afternoon, plenty of time to continue their journey for several more miles. Puzzled she turned to Robert. 'Is this the place we intend to stay tonight? Could we not continue longer?'

He shook his head. 'No, you are supposed to be injured. Which reminds me, you had better put your arm back into the sling before we get there. Your stepfather would not expect us to have travelled any further than this. Remember, we have already cantered a considerable distance which they would not have been in a position to do.'

'Of course, I had not thought of that. Also, I must begin to call you Dudley, and you to address me as *my dear*.'

He smiled. 'I think as we are supposed to be married, you could address me by my given name, which is . . . ' He paused, as if not sure which name to give her. 'It makes no difference, but his name is Simon, you already know that mine is Robert. As long as I don't refer to you as Annabel, we shall not come unstuck.'

He fell back in order to speak to George without being overheard and then came back to her side. 'The boy will go in and get things organized for us, I should like to ride a little further down the road with you.'

She made no objection, but was puzzled by his suggestion. They rode past a substantial house, several pretty cottages, a blacksmiths, a general stores and milliners, then on the outskirts of the village where there were a few tumbledown hovels and a church.

'I thought you might like to spend a short time here; it must be many years since you have had the opportunity to go inside such a building.'

How thoughtful of him. She would dearly love to pay her respects to her Maker, and say prayers for the success of their plan. She beamed at him, wondering why she had ever thought him insensitive. 'Thank you, I should like that very much. Are you coming with me, or do you remain with the horses?'

He looked uncomfortable, but replied with a small smile. 'I shall remain out here for a moment, to give you time alone, I will join you shortly.'

'There is something that has been bothering me, who exactly does George think I am? He must have known there was only one lady in our party.'

'Good God! Did we not tell you? He is not party to the deception, he thinks you to be Lady Sophia.'

She shook her head in disbelief. 'In which case he must believe my arm has made a miraculous recovery, I have been using it freely all day.'

He grinned. 'It's immaterial either way; by the time he returns from this jaunt your mother and Dudley will be long gone and their pursuers following us.'

He dismounted and lifted her from the saddle, it was awkward dismounting with her arm in a sling. He escorted her to the church door and opened it, then stepped aside to allow her to enter alone.

It took a few moments for her eyes to adjust to the gloom. It was an ancient building, with a magnificent stained-glass window, one of the few that escaped destruction when Oliver Cromwell had been in power. Revelling in the hallowed atmosphere, she walked to the altar rail at the front of the church, bowed her head in reverence then entered the front pew. Kneeling on the stone floor she began her prayers.

So lost in her communion with God she was startled by the sound of voices outside. The church door opened. Hastily regaining her feet, she turned to see Robert accompanied by a gentleman dressed sombrely. Who might he be?

The man walked past her into the vestry, leaving her to whisper to Robert. 'Who is that? Am I not supposed to be in here?'

He guided her back until she was standing in the empty space at the rear of the church where the poorer folk stood during services. 'He's the vicar, my dear, he has come to marry us.'

Without his support she would have collapsed at his feet. 'Marry us? Now? I had thought you'd forgotten about it, that it was no longer necessary. I'm not sure that I wish to be married to you, that I wish to be married at all.' She was babbling, not making any sense, and looked frantically from side to side, hoping there was a way she could escape from this.

Gently he drew her closer, so close the heat from his body warmed her. 'Sweetheart, you have no choice. I have the licence, we must be married, there is no alternative. It's what we decided, what you agreed.'

She shook her head, tried to extricate herself from his grip but he tightened his hold and spoke urgently, his words breathed into her ear. 'Do you think your mother would have allowed us to ride off like this unchaperoned, to share a bedchamber tonight, if she had not known I intended to marry you this afternoon? It is difficult enough for her to be obliged to share accommodation with a man to whom she is not married, it would break her heart if the same were to happen to her beloved daughter.'

She stopped struggling. He was right, whatever her feelings, it would destroy her mama if she did not marry. She would not think of the future, but only of today, that the marriage would keep her safe, and make her mother happy.

He relaxed his hold and moved a few

inches away. Angrily she brushed away her tears and faced him. 'I shall do it, reluctantly, with grave reservations about the outcome, but I will not let my mother down.'

Something flashed in his eyes, was it triumph or relief? Too soon, he slipped his arm in hers and guided her to the altar where the vicar was waiting to perform the marriage ceremony. Witnesses! Robert had forgotten that they needed two witnesses, the marriage would not be legal without their marks on the certificate. The church door opened and closed softly behind them and she knew he had not forgotten, there were others present. She did not look over her shoulder to see who they were. Her fate was sealed by their appearance.

★ ★ ★

Sir Randolph found the apartment to his satisfaction and after changing his clothes, returned downstairs to find that the butler was waiting to escort him to the dining-room.

The table had been laid for one, Hughes was obviously dining elsewhere. He enjoyed the meal, demanded two bottles of claret and carried the port decanter with him when he left. He was determined to find somewhere more convivial than the vast drawing-room, to sit in for the remainder of the evening.

Eventually he discovered the library, the fire was laid but not lit. It was the work of moments to ignite it from his candle. Then he walked round the room lighting the other candlesticks until the room was bathed in a golden glow.

The book-lined walls reminded him of home. He rarely read the books in his library but owning them made him feel intelligent. Whilst he waited for the fire to burn more brightly he wandered to the leather-topped desk where there were several letters in a tray waiting to be answered. Idly he picked up the first. It was a bill from the local milliners and there were several others in similar vein, but at the bottom of the pile was one that interested him.

As he read it his eyes blazed with fury. He had been sent on a fool's errand, the guests staying at Brandon Manor were strangers to him. This letter was a confirmation of their arrival, it was Lady Barton's godmother and her husband she had gone out with.

Forgetting he was not at home, he hurled the books, candlesticks and other oddments from the surface with one sweep of his arm. The resulting crash brought the sound of running feet towards him. The door was flung open and the butler, flanked by two footmen, viewed the carnage open-mouthed.

Before the butler could retreat he strode across the room and grabbed him by his cravat. 'Tell me, what is Major Dudley to Lady Barton?'

The man could barely speak as he choked the air from his lungs. 'He is her brother, he visited here with Colonel Sinclair last week.'

He slackened his grip allowing the man to gulp a breath before tightening his fingers once more. 'Where does Dudley live?'

The man did not answer fast enough and he shook him like a terrier shakes a rat. 'Tell me, or it shall be the worse for you.'

Before he received an answer something unprecedented occurred. The two footmen sprang forward and seized him by the shoulders.

'That's enough of that. Don't you handle Mr Foster so roughly,' the larger footman said.

He was being manhandled by a member of the lower orders! He was incandescent with rage.

'Hughes, where are you? Get in here at once.' His shout was loud enough to echo throughout the house.

Foster, still gasping for breath, spoke sharply to his two underlings. 'You'd best release the gentleman, but fetch his bags and rouse his servants, he'll not stay here another moment. He is no friend of Lady Barton's of that I'm quite certain.'

The next moment Randolph was flat on his back, the door slammed and the key turned outside. They had dared to push him over! They were servants; it was their job to do what they were bid, not to attack their masters in this way. Heavy footsteps heralded the arrival, he hoped, of Hughes and his other men. The door opened and they gaped at him.

He scrambled to his feet, his cheeks flushed with anger and embarrassment at having been found in such a humiliating position. He reached inside his jacket pocket and pulled out his pistol, at once the three men followed suit.

'The servants turned on me; they intend to throw us out, but that will not happen. We shall round them up and lock them in the cellar. Their mistress can release them when she returns tomorrow.'

★　★　★

Just before Hughes closed the cellar door, Randolph reached in and grabbed the butler once again. 'You did not have the opportunity to tell me what I wish to know. If you wish to survive this encounter you will answer me. Whereabouts does Major Dudley have his estate?' He levelled the gun, the barrel inches from the old man's face.

'Norwich, he has a place outside Norwich. Bracksted House. I don't know the exact direction but you could ask, anyone will tell you where it's situated.'

Randolph threw the man backwards, not caring if he broke his neck on the stairs. Hughes bolted the door. 'There, we have them now. We shall leave first thing in the morning. Is the house secure? I don't want the outside staff to know what is going on in here.'

'All right and tight, sir, exactly as you instructed. They will have plenty to occupy them what with the maids being in with the menservants.'

★ ★ ★

The church was quiet, Annabel thought Robert might hear her heart it was thudding so loudly. The vicar cleared his throat and before she had time to think about it a gold band was pushed on to the ring finger of her left hand. She was committed for better or worse to honour and obey until one of them die.

The vicar cleared his throat again. It was an annoying habit. 'If you would care to wait with your wife, I shall fill in the certificate, enter it in the parish register and get the witnesses to put their marks. Congratulations on your marriage, Colonel Sinclair. I hope you both will be very happy.'

That would never be. What hope was there for true happiness in an arrangement like this? Love on one side of the union was not sufficient to ensure the happiness of both partners.

He sensed her disquiet, made no attempt to embrace her, to give her the traditional bridal kiss. 'Come along, my dear, why don't you wait outside in the fresh air, until he brings the paper?'

She nodded dumbly. Somehow she completed the long walk to the door without her knees giving way. The church appeared empty, the witnesses had obviously gone into the vestry with the vicar.

The horses were grazing contentedly. Silver raised his massive head, whickering a greeting. She ran to him, throwing her arms around his neck, drenching his mane with her tears. This was not how it should have been. Mama had told her so many times about her real father, how much in love they had been, how she had given up everything to be with him.

234

Annabel had given up everything, but not because she loved Robert, but for love of her mama. Her love for him was too new to survive this hasty marriage. It would shrivel and die in such circumstances. He was coming, hastily she dried her tears on her sleeve. She needed to be calm to ask him this favour. She turned. He was standing behind her his eyes alert and watchful.

'Colonel . . . ' She hesitated, perhaps if she had addressed him less formally it would be better. 'Robert, all this has been a shock to me. I scarcely know you, this is not how I thought my wedding would be, without even my mama here to wish us well.'

'I know what you're trying to say, sweetheart. Please do not distress yourself, I have already given my word to Lady Sophia. This shall be a marriage in name only until you wish to make it otherwise.' His voice rang with sincerity and she believed him. Was she relieved or disappointed that he was prepared to forego the pleasures of the marriage bed?

17

Annabel and Robert walked the short distance from the church to The White Horse. George was waiting in the cobbled yard to receive the horses, the landlord was standing in the doorway beaming.

'Here, boy, when you have untacked our horses bring the bags to our rooms.'

George touched his forelock. 'I'll do that, sir. It's a right nice place here, and they keep a good kitchen the ostler told me.'

During this brief conversation Robert had kept hold of her hand. She didn't like to create a scene by tugging it free. From his knowing looks it was obvious the landlord knew they were just married. 'Come on in, sir, madam. I have two fine rooms put by for you, and as instructed a bath is being drawn as we speak.'

Her spirits lifted a little. A bath? How long was it since she'd had the luxury of immersing herself completely in warm water? She shivered. She had no maid with her, did her new husband intend to stand in that role? He had said he wouldn't demand to share her bed, but had said nothing about keeping his distance in other ways.

Upstairs the rooms were more than adequate, the huge tester bed, with lavender-scented linen, was made up and ready. A roaring apple log fire burned merrily, and in front of it, luxury of luxuries, a hip bath, hiding behind a black lacquered screen. She ran forward in delight.

'This is the best wedding present I could have had.' She dipped her finger to discover the water was piping hot. 'I shall make use of this first . . . er . . . Robert, if you do not mind. There's a more than adequate parlour you can sit in for the moment.' It was best to get this matter settled straightaway. She stared belligerently and he laughed out loud.

'Don't ruffle your feathers, my little bantam hen, I have no intention of remaining in here. You shall have your privacy.' He sauntered to the door, turning as he reached it. 'Please feel free to call me if you need any assistance. As you have no maid, it is possible you might encounter some difficulties removing your garments.'

His hateful chuckling remained with her after the door shut. She would remove her riding habit without assistance, and certainly not with *his* help, or die in the attempt. First she must take off her boots and that was no mean task without anything to hook them over. She tried jamming them on the edge of the fender to no avail. Her fingers were now covered in mud, and both boots were still firmly *in situ*. She would have to go next door and ask for his assistance, much as it annoyed her to do so.

He was lounging on the *chaise-longue*, his jacket removed, his shirtsleeves remarkably white considering everything that had taken place.

'I cannot remove my boots, would you do so for me? Please.' She knew she sounded ungrateful, but the prospect of him taking her feet in his hands filled her with trepidation. He swung his legs to the floor, a wicked glint in his eye.

'Turn around, my love, and present me with your boot heel.' He grasped the heel and with one tug the boot slid off. She presented the second and he removed it with equal ease.

'Thank you, Robert. I believe I can manage the rest myself.' He solemnly handed her the boots.

'I am looking forward to taking a bath myself, sweetheart, call me when you've done.' He stretched lazily. 'As you can see I do not have much more to take off.'

Her face scarlet, she ran into the bedroom, slamming the door. How could he mention something as indelicate as removing his garments? The image *that* presented was almost too much for her composure. She paused, fingers resting on the buttons at the waist of her habit. She had never seen a man unclothed; Fred had never removed his shirt even in the hottest weather. She wondered if Robert had scars anywhere on his person from his years of soldiering. Were his chest and shoulders as tanned as his face and forearms?

She tingled all over. Perhaps it would be in order for her to assist *him*, after all did not wives do so in olden days? What nonsense! She must not think of such things. She had only known him for two weeks and she was speculating in a most unseemly manner. She was not certain married women ever viewed their husbands naked. Mama had told her a gentleman wore a nightshirt in bed.

What was wrong with her? Hadn't she decided to remain aloof until he came to love her? Desire was *not* the same at all. With the slightest encouragement he would . . . she pushed the thought back. Hadn't this sort of thing placed her in danger from her stepfather?

Fortunately her garments all fastened at the front and very soon she was stepping into the water. She had left her hair in its usual plait around her head, believing it would not be sensible to attempt to wash that as well as her person. Mama always helped with such a task; she had never attempted it alone.

The bath was not long enough for her to stretch out. She giggled; he would have to sit with his knees almost under his chin when he got in. However, it was deep and she could submerge herself leaving only her knees peeping out of the water. It was bliss, the warm water soothed her aching limbs. Her eyes closed. No, she must not fall asleep, he might become impatient and barge in to demand his turn.

She sponged herself all over, but by then her hair was wet — she might as well wash it after all. Scrambling on to her knees she plunged her head in and rubbed the lemon soap over her locks. She rinsed it at the far end of the bath, where the water was still relatively clear of suds.

Satisfied her ablutions had made her sweet smelling, the tang of the stable finally removed, she stepped out. Snatching the biggest of the three bath sheets that were warming in front of the fire she enveloped herself.

It was so voluminous it trailed behind her. A second smaller cloth she twisted around her hair like a turban. She felt wonderful, relaxed and warm. She gazed in dismay at the scummy water in the bath. How could he be expected to share that? She had not realized how dirty she had been.

Would the kitchen have the resources to refill the bath? She must ring and ask them immediately if they would do so. There was another screen at the far side of the room behind which she could change. She looked around for her bag.

Good grief! It had not arrived from the stable yard. Unless she was prepared to put back on her mired clothes she would have to remain wrapped in towels. This was an unmitigated disaster. There was not even a robe she could put on. Where was the wretched boy? Why did he not appear with her bag?

There was no option, she must go and ask Robert to fetch it for her. As far as she could see there was no bell strap in the bedchamber, it must be in the sitting-room. Holding tightly to the towel, she crossed the room and peered around the door. Her husband was stretched out on the daybed, but his eyes were closed, his stockinged feet resting on the upholstery. He appeared to be asleep.

Botheration! Now what? 'Robert, Robert, I need your assistance. Please wake up this instant.'

There was no reaction from the figure

stretched out so comfortably. She opened the door wider and put her head round further.

'Wake up, I need to speak to you urgently.' Still no reaction. He sighed and stirred a little, but that was all. She must go in and shake him by the shoulder. Holding the towel close she tiptoed over and was stretching out a finger when his eyes opened. Disconcerted, she froze. The wretched man had been awake all along.

Angrily she stepped away treading on the trailing end of the towel and even his quick reactions could not prevent her from tumbling backwards.

★ ★ ★

Robert could hear his wife splashing about in the water and wondered at what point in the procedure would Annabel realize she had nothing clean to put on? He pushed the bags further under the daybed with his foot, stretched out his stockinged feet and relaxed. Would she come to him and demand that he fetch her clothes? Or would she reappear dressed in soiled garments?

She was far too fond of giving orders, expecting him to be at her beck and call. He had promised to stay out of her bed, but that did not mean he was going to allow her to ignore her other marriage vows. She had promised to cherish, honour and obey — and he intended she should do exactly that.

It was taking an unconscionably long time for one woman to have a bath. His lips curved as he recalled her yesterday when she was dressed as an urchin, face filthy, and hands even worse. Had she washed her hair? A flood of heat surged round him. The first time he had seen her, her golden tresses tumbling over her shoulders, he'd known she was the most desirable woman he had ever seen. He had not changed his mind, in fact it was going to be damned difficult keeping his promise.

His heart remained frozen; he could not love her but he could *make* love to her. Hopefully this would be enough for both of them.

He loved to see her eyes flash with anger. Annabel was the only person, male or female, who had the courage to stand up to him. He was anticipating a tempestuous marriage. He closed his eyes, letting his thoughts drift. Was it her spirit or her beauty and intelligence that attracted him? It had been seeing her tumbling off her horse outside Brandon Manor that had pierced his heart, made him certain he could marry her and not regret it.

He stared at the closed door which lay

between them. How long could he keep away from her? He had given his word, but if she changed her mind he would not hold back. Lady Sophia could not expect him to hold to his promise if Annabel wished to become his true wife. He settled back. Many marriages started with affection only, maybe not even that. Perhaps after time real love would come — until then physical love would have to suffice.

The unmistakable sound of her climbing out of the bath alerted him. He forced his limbs to relax, feigning sleep. The door opened and she called. He ignored her. She called again. She sounded so cross, now she would have to come in and wake him up.

As she approached he could scarcely contain his amusement, then the warmth from her newly bathed skin filled his nostrils. Something quite different drove him. She must be within arm's reach. He opened his eyes and his jaw dropped. He could not prevent his expression showing how he felt.

She wasn't dressed at all. There was a towel around her head hiding her hair. The one around her body left her white shoulders and slender arms clearly visible. He hardened, his arousal would be visible without his jacket to disguise it. He jack-knifed and his sudden movement caused her to step backwards.

His lightning reactions failed him and she tumbled to the floor. The towel she had so carefully wrapped about her person began to unravel. He dared not move; if he did he would break his promise and take her into the bedroom and make love to her.

★ ★ ★

The intensity of Robert's gaze pinned her to the floor. For a moment she couldn't get her limbs to respond. Then abruptly he turned away, releasing her. She grabbed the corners of the towel and attempted to scramble to her feet. The more she tried to get up the more tangled she became. To make matters worse, the towel around her head unrolled and added to the chaos.

She had to get out of there, she was crimson from her toes to her crown. She had revealed parts of her anatomy that even her mother had not seen since she was grown. With a strangled sob of frustration she tried to keep herself decent, push her wet hair out of the way, and stand up without treading on the end of the enormous bath sheet.

'Keep still, sweetheart, your struggles are making matters worse. Let me help you. No, don't flinch away from me, I'm your husband, you have nothing to be embarrassed about.' His voice was gentle, reassuring and in no way predatory.

She stilled and he enfolded her in his arms and swept her up as if she weighed nothing at all. Kicking the unwanted towel to one side he carried her back into the bedroom, placing her on the bed.

'Sit there. I have your bag in the other room. I shall bring it through to you.'

She shivered, not sure if it was cold or anticipation that shook her so violently. She felt vulnerable sitting alone in the centre of the vast bed, as if inviting his attentions. Then he returned and dropped her bag beside her.

'Look at you, you look like a drowned rat. Get some clothes on and then come next door and I shall dry your hair for you.'

He spoke as if to a small child, and she smiled back. 'Thank you, Robert. The water is not only filthy I believe it will be cold by now. If you wish to take a bath you will have to send for fresh water.'

'I shall do that, but not to worry if I don't get my bath tonight, I shall have one another time.'

The door closed. With chattering teeth she removed the wet bath sheet and rummaged for her undergarments. Once she had these safely on, she relaxed. Her blue dress was sadly creased, but was better than the other garment she had brought with her. She required new clothes, perhaps now it would be safe to go back to Brandon Hall and replenish her wardrobe.

Annabel had no idea what was going to happen after the expected confrontation with her stepfather. Would they go and live in Hertfordshire, or remain at Brandon Hall? She would have to ask Robert.

She drew her dress over her head, did up the tiny matching buttons and tied the sash. Hanging the wet towels over the rail, she collected a hairbrush and the last dry towel. As she entered the sitting-room she saw the flicker of a skirt as a maid disappeared. Robert turned back to her and smiled. Her stomach somersaulted. He was undeniably handsome, and when he looked at her like that, she responded without wishing to.

There were cushions piled on the floor, the day bed was moved around to run parallel to the fireplace. He gestured towards the cushions. 'Sit there, my dear girl. It must be tedious having hair of such a length.'

'I had thought of having it cut off, shall I do so?'

'Over my dead body. Your hair is your crowning glory; it is what I first noticed about you.'

She folded herself on the cushions and he

sat behind, his legs forming a warm cradle. He reached round her and began to rub her hair dry.

'Are they bringing a fresh bath? I feel really guilty having used all the water myself.'

'It seems that the copper is already filled with hot water. They will come and take away the old in the next half an hour. I've also ordered food to be brought. I'm ravenous, I don't know about you.'

'I am indeed, I do hope they will take care of George. Though, I must admit, I had excellent food when I was a stable boy for two days.'

He chuckled. 'I'm sure he will be well looked after — he'd better be, I'm paying them enough.'

The sound of buckets and banging came from the bedroom, there must obviously be a servant's entrance somewhere in that chamber she had not discovered. She settled back against him and he picked up her hair brush. Taking a section he began brushing out the tangles. She hung her head forward, draping her hair over her face in order to receive the warmth from the logs.

The room was quiet, not a strained silence, more companionable. Perhaps this marriage would not be as bad as she had feared. It was rather pleasant to have someone to take care of *her* for a change. Not that dear Mama did not do her best, but she had always been more interested in her art than domestic matters. Ever since they had lived at Brandon Hall it had been Annabel's job to organize the house and garden with the help of the Hopkins family.

A bang on the door interrupted them. 'That must be our food. If you would be so kind as to lay it out on the table I shall go and braid my hair, I think it is dry enough to do so.'

She didn't wait for his reply. In the bedroom two chambermaids were tipping the last of the clean water into the bath.

'There you are, madam, all done. Major Dudley can take his bath now.'

The two girls giggled and nudged each other, staring at her unbound hair, crumpled gown and bare feet. She had not bothered to find stockings when she had dressed earlier.

'There's fresh towels on the rail, madam, but I don't expect you'll need all three.'

Giggling and pushing each other, they vanished through the hidden door at the far side of the room.

Whatever were they sniggering about? She viewed the towels, and the water and for a moment didn't comprehend. Then it dawned. They had seen her hair, her feet, and believed that she would be remaining in the room whilst he bathed. That they would be tumbling into bed at any moment to celebrate their union.

Maybe that wasn't such a bad idea. He had just dried her hair, should she not reciprocate in some way? The water was deep enough to cover him waist high, and if she knelt behind him she could soap his back and wash his hair. If she did this she would finally get to see what a naked man looked like. Did she have the courage to attempt it?

18

Robert spoke softly from behind her. 'Let me do that for you, sweetheart, after all we're already married.'

Without waiting for her permission he began to braid her hair efficiently. His eyes met hers in the mirror and a strange warmth pooled in her nether regions. He made her feel so odd, her limbs no longer belonged to her, it was as if she was someone else entirely.

His hands were brushing the back of her neck as he arranged her hair. He reached out to take the ribbon and when his fingers touched hers they were cool. Or was it that hers were burning for some reason? She cleared her throat.

'Your bath's ready, Robert. I'm quite capable of plaiting my own hair. As soon as it's done I shall go and wait in the parlour.'

He ignored her. Having completed one side he deftly fixed the ribbon around the end. 'If that's what you want, my love. Why don't you leave it as it is? Don't bother to wind it round your head, leave it down. Like this, it reminds me of paintings I have seen of olden times, fair maidens attending to their menfolk.'

He had read her mind. Flushing painfully she jerked her head away and completed the task herself, looking anywhere but at him. Her former wanton thoughts about helping him with his ablutions evaporated. She was not a sophisticated lady, was out of her depth when it came to matters of this sort. If she wasn't careful she would find herself agreeing to becoming his true wife, to sharing his bed. She had tied a ribbon around her plait many times before but this time her fingers fumbled and it took several attempts to tie the bow.

Annabel was about to stand when she heard the unmistakable sound of him stepping into the bath. He had not waited for her to leave, had deliberately removed his clothes to see how she would react. The air crackled with tension; she gripped the edge of the table and took several steadying breaths.

She would *not* be embarrassed, she was his wife, had the right to be in here with him. Despite her nervousness she half smiled, after all, had he not seen all of *her* when she had tumbled and her towels had parted?

In one graceful movement she rose, but kept her eyes fixed firmly somewhere above where she thought his head would be. Eye contact could prove disastrous. How silly — he could not sit facing her, the hip bath was not built to allow that. He would have his back to her, it would be quite safe to glance at him.

His head and shoulders protruded above the rim of the bath. His skin was a creamy colour below his neck, his back muscly, his shoulders broad. There were no scars to mar his perfection.

He had not picked up a fresh bar of soap or the washcloth. He was jammed into the bath, could not possibly turn round and touch her. Should she do it? Yes, it was time to show him she was no child, that this was a partnership of adults.

She glided across to pick up the soap and flannel and then paused behind him. He was aware of her presence and he shifted uncomfortably in the water as if he had cramp.

'I thought that I could wash your back if you would like me to do so.'

A kind of strangled groan came from him and, certain he was unwell, she dropped to his side, instinctively reaching out to hold his shoulder.

'Don't touch me. Leave this room at once, I wish to bathe alone.'

She scrambled to her feet in shock. Flinging the soap and flannel at his head she fled from the room, not sure what she had done to make him so angry. His reaction renewed her fear that she had married a man with an uncertain temper.

The supper was still on two trays at the far side of the room. When her legs were able to carry her safely she busied herself setting out two places on a nearby table. She felt sick. Why had he turned against her like that? She did not understand him at all.

The aroma of hot vegetable soup wafted from the tureen and her stomach rumbled. The sound of splashing next door indicated he was still occupied. She would not wait for him to join her. He was bound to make her lose her appetite again and the food would be far tastier eaten hot.

First ladling herself a bowl of soup, next she piled a plate with venison, chutney, cheese and bread and carried it across to the window seat. The tray made an adequate table set across her lap.

She didn't raise her head when the door opened; he did not deserve her attention having been so unpleasant. After all, she had been only offering to help him, there was no reason for him to have snarled at her.

'I see you have made a start, is the soup as delicious as it sounds?'

Her spoon stopped in mid-air. Had she been making so much noise? She couldn't stop herself smiling. 'It is, and if you don't take some, I shall eat the rest myself.'

He chuckled and the atmosphere between them was once more convivial. As his wife she supposed she would have to get used to his mercurial moods. They were over quickly, and he had not shown himself to be a violent man in any other way.

There had been a jug of ale provided for him and butter-milk for her. When she had completed her meal she was quite ready to forgive him for his earlier incivility.

She stood up, brushing the debris from her lap, wiping her mouth on a linen square. She took her tray to the table by the door. 'That was quite delicious, I feel so much better now. When you've finished, I shall ring for them to remove the trays.'

'Do it now, by the time they get here I shall have done.'

When the maid arrived Annabel asked for the bath to be removed as well. 'Those poor girls, they have done nothing but carry buckets up and down stairs all afternoon just so we can be clean.'

'You're too soft-hearted, my love. They're paid to do such tasks and think nothing of it.'

He tossed a few logs on the fire whilst she curled up on the daybed, tucking her bare feet into the folds of her skirt in order to hide them. He was settled comfortably in the armchair opposite, in a clean shirt that was as crumpled as her own gown, britches and, like her, no stockings.

For some reason the bodice of her dress began to feel uncomfortably tight as she stared at his long feet, seeing the strength in his toes, the corded muscles of his ankles. Why should a gentleman's feet affect her in this way? She needed to think of other things, more mundane matters before she lost her composure.

'Robert, where shall we live when all this business with Sir Randolph is over?'

'Wherever you wish. I have an estate in Hertfordshire as you know, but I am an absentee landlord, I have an excellent estate manager and the property is let until next summer. I could take a place in London, we could return to Brandon Hall, or we could travel abroad for a few months.'

'I have always longed to visit Italy, to see the ancient ruins for myself. I understand the light is clear there, and warm all year round. Mama would love to live in Italy. She is an artist, you know, the money she has earned from selling her paintings have brought us a few extras these past years.'

'That does not surprise me, she has a bohemian air about her. Italy it shall be, my love. My perambulations around the Continent did not include that country. I didn't have a grand tour, I joined the army when I finished my education. Excellent. That is settled, and when we return do you wish me to arrange for the tenant to remove himself from my property? Or shall we live at Brandon Hall?'

'Brandon Hall — at least, at first. It's a lovely part of the country, and the house would be so comfortable if there was money to spend on it. We already have Mary and her family to organize things for us.' She clapped her hands to her mouth in horror. 'Do you know, I have not thought about Billy, Fred or old Tom these past few days. How were they when you returned?'

'Doing well. Billy was up and about, Fred staying in bed reluctantly, and even old Tom was able to take food. However, I think it will be some weeks before he's back to normal.' The noises from next door had finally ceased, the bath and its contents removed. He glanced at the door and then back to her, his face serious.

'My love, there are things we need to talk about, and you must listen carefully, and promise not to interrupt.'

'Is something wrong?' She remembered his annoyance when she had offered to wash

257

him, and felt her cheeks redden.

'Exactly so, my love. Your mother should have told you all this long ago. Do you know what takes place between a man and a woman when they make love?'

Her eyes widened in shock. She shook her head, her throat too tight to answer.

'I thought not. Have you seen farmyard beasts mating in the spring?'

Her cheeks flaming, she nodded, too embarrassed to look at him. Whatever had possessed him to discuss such intimate matters with her?

'It is roughly the same process for humankind. When a man desires a woman there are changes to his anatomy that make this act a possibility.'

Changes in anatomy? She knew men were built differently, had seen the male parts of her gelding, but had never thought about it in relation to a man. She couldn't help herself, her eyes were drawn to the area he mentioned. There was a definite bulge at the junction of his legs. To her astonishment it began to grow. She could not look away — what was happening to him?

Suddenly he was beside her, his arms around her waist, his mouth covering hers. It was nothing like their previous two kisses. His mouth was hard and demanding, his tongue slid across her lips sending frissons of exquisite pleasure through her body. A delicious heat began to rise from her toes until it centred in a most unusual place.

Her mouth opened allowing him to invade its moist depths, she wanted something from him, but did not know what it was. They fell back on to the *chaise-longue* and there was something hard pressing against her stomach. Finally Annabel understood what he had been talking about.

It was as though a bucket of ice had been tipped over her head. All desire vanished to be replaced by a feeling of panic. Frantically she pushed at his chest, turning her head away. 'Let me go, you must not. You promised, let me go at once.'

Instantly she was free and he was standing by the window, his cheeks were hectic, his eyes dark, his expression almost unrecognizable. He turned his back, leaning his face against the window pane. From his rigidity she thought he must be angry again. No, not angry, Robert was in pain. Whatever happened to a man's anatomy must obviously be painful. She still didn't quite understand why this should be so, and had no intention of asking.

She could not bear the thought of having her body invaded in that way, had no intention of behaving like an animal from the farmyard. If he wished to do that sort of thing then he must find himself a mistress. The thought of what took place between a man and a woman brought back the hideous memories. Her mother's screams were engraved on her memory, she could not let herself be used in that way.

'I'm sorry if I disappointed you, but I do not wish to be your wife in that way. I understood that it would be an arrangement of convenience only. A gentleman would not break his word and try to persuade me to do otherwise.'

Not waiting for him to reply she returned to the bedchamber, pushing the bolt across. She no longer trusted him not to come in and get into her bed. She leant against the door, recalling the sensations she had experienced when he kissed her, when his hands had caressed her body. No matter how pleasurable this had been she did not want to consummate the union.

Loving him was not enough — she needed to know he felt the same. If he truly loved her he would never treat her badly. Now she understood why he had shouted out when she'd offered to wash his back. Just having her close by seemed to make him want to ravish her.

She shuddered. Men were no better than animals. She must remain with him until she was of age, and then demand to have the marriage annulled and seek her independence. Wherever Major Dudley and her mother were hiding, she would find them and make her life at their side.

★ ★ ★

Sir Randolph decided he must quit Brandon Manor at dawn. One of the outside servants might well call out the militia when they realized he had incarcerated the entire indoor staff at gunpoint in the cellar. Both carriages were waiting outside, the two bullyboys and the maid already in the second.

'Hughes, do you have any idea on the whereabouts of Norwich?'

'I questioned one of the grooms, sir, the Norwich Road is the one we turned off to come here. It's signposted about two miles from here.'

'We'll catch them up at some point. I only wish to take my wife and her daughter, get your men to dispose of everybody else. I want no witnesses to the abduction.'

The coach trundled off down the drive, Hughes slumped in his habitual position on one side, he in his corner on the other. It was strange, where had this Major Dudley appeared from? Brandon Hall was at the back of beyond, and Sophia and Annabel had not been out in society or he would have found them earlier. He shrugged, he cared not about such matters. In fact, he realized, he cared not about the fact that his wife had been unfaithful to him. Annabel would still be an innocent and that was all that mattered. He intended to be the one to initiate her in the arts of the bedroom. His wife would live the life of a nun from now on, he would keep her locked away. It would be revenge enough her knowing what was happening to her beloved daughter and that she was helpless to prevent it.

He checked his pistol was still primed and ready, and heard Hughes do the same. Whoever this Dudley person was, he would die for his temerity.

★ ★ ★

Annabel tossed and turned all night, expecting at any moment to hear a thunderous knocking on the door. This did not happen. She was left undisturbed and, by the early hours felt decidedly guilty about her cavalier treatment of him.

The fire had burned out, the chamber was

chill, and she had left him in his shirt and britches, with no blankets to cover him. She crept out of bed and removed the thick cover she had pushed to one side during the night. It was still pitch dark outside; she was sure it was several hours till dawn. At least Robert could be warm for the remainder of the night.

She lit a candle from the embers. With the coverlet draped over one arm she unbolted the door. The room was dark. No, not quite, the fire in here was still burning.

Should she go in, or just throw the blanket in his direction and retreat hastily?

'Are you coming in, my dear, or shall you remain dithering in the doorway indefinitely?'

The voice coming from the darkness caused her to stub her toe painfully on the door jamb. Her nervousness turned instantly to annoyance. 'You frightened me, and now I have hurt my toe. To think I was worried about you being cold and was bringing you an extra blanket.'

The sound of his chuckles filled the room. 'I am a soldier, sweetheart, this is the height of luxury to me. But you have brought me a blanket, I think it's a kind thought.' His voice sobered. 'You're quite safe to come in, my love. There will not be a repeat of last night's incident. You were right to castigate me, I took shameful advantage of you. It will not happen again. Now, do I get that blanket or am I to remain shivering in my shirt for the remainder of the night?'

No longer scared, she hurried forward dropping the blanket into his lap. 'There you are, Robert. I have hardly slept a wink, I do not like to be at odds with you. Can we still be friends?' Her eyes were now accustomed to the gloom, his white shirt glowed in the darkness.

'I understand. When we know each other better, perhaps we can talk about your feelings. You might wish to do so one day. I was a brute to try and seduce you. My only excuse is that I find you a most desirable woman. It is becoming increasingly difficult for me to keep my distance.'

Hastily she stepped away. 'In which case, sir, I shall make sure I do not come within arm's reach, and will endeavour to remain as uninviting as I can.'

'My dear girl, even dressed as a smelly stable lad, I still wanted you in my bed.'

He was doing it again. She felt her cheeks glow, and a languor claimed her limbs. Why an experienced man of the world should find her so attractive was a complete mystery. Wasn't it her stepfather's evil intentions towards her that had caused her mother to flee in the first place? Sir Randolph must also see something that she did not. The idea that both men should be motivated by the same base desires filled her with dismay.

She stared at her husband. 'I am sorry that you feel this way, Robert, but it's none of my doing. In my opinion all men are beasts, I want none of them. I'm afraid that you must learn to control your base instincts.' Something prompted her to continue. 'And as far as I'm concerned, if you wish to do *that* sort of thing, I suggest you find yourself a willing mistress. You will not get that from me, not now, not ever.'

19

The door closed with a bang and Robert's fingers clenched. God dammit! It was all his fault. He should not have forced the issue, then she would still trust him and he could have taken his time and gently wooed her. Now she saw him as some kind of monster. What had the poor girl been exposed to when she was young? Something had happened that had given her a fear of intimacy. It was that bastard Rushton who was to blame: he had curdled her mind, turned something pleasurable and natural into an abomination.

Whatever she might think he could never be unfaithful. He had lived in celibacy before, could do so again. Their union would be consummated eventually. Annabel would learn to trust him, her natural instincts would overcome her disgust and he would be able to show her how wonderful physical love could be.

He was going to be patient until that moment arrived. He wanted her too much to give up. He smiled, no doubt she thought to claim an annulment in due course. He would never agree to it. He stretched out. In spite of his protests that he was a hardened soldier, it had become decidedly cold in the sitting-room and the blanket was most welcome.

Robert did not stir again until the door opened and Annabel stood there, dressed in her mother's riding habit, eyes snapping, angrily gesturing to him to get up.

'Do you intend to lie there all day? We should have left some time ago. I have been ready this past hour. I could not wait for you to stir any longer.' Annabel glared at him. Did he realize how important it was to be on their way, to put distance between themselves and their pursuers?

He rubbed his bristly chin and grinned, unrepentant. 'Am I not to have my breakfast before we leave?'

Her boot tapped the floor. 'I am going down to make sure the horses are waiting for us. If you are not ready, I shall leave without you.'

★   ★   ★

His laughter followed her down the passage. Why did he not take her seriously? She met the landlord in the entrance hall and he bowed politely.

'Shall you be wanting anything to eat before you leave, madam?'

'No, thank you, we shall be leaving soon as my husband is ready.'

Outside the yard was busy, the overnight guests preparing to depart. Where was George? She could hardly march round to the stable and demand to speak to him. Then she spotted him leading Silver.

'We must leave immediately. Are the other horses ready?'

'They are, madam. I just need the bags to tie on. I shall bring the others round.' He tethered Silver to the rail.

At last. Robert was coming — they could depart.

They had been travelling a mile or two when she decided he was forgiven for his tardiness.

'How far is it to Norwich, Robert? Or should I be calling you Dudley?' She smiled. 'Do I still have to pretend I have a broken arm and that I am my mother?'

'No, it no longer matters. You are safe from Rushton.'

'George's so confused by our odd behaviour that he refers to me as madam, not using any name at all.'

'I'm paying him well enough for each day he is with us for him to accept whatever happens without comment.'

They had set out later than expected and it

was now almost noon. Several carriages drove by in both directions. They had just passed through a tollgate and were riding along a deserted strip of road, when they heard the sound of a carriage approaching at a reckless speed.

'Into the trees. Do it. Now.'

She didn't hesitate, wrenching at her horse's head to turn him from the road, kicking the animal again so that it broke into a gallop. She heard Robert shout to George to abandon the baggage horse and follow them. They raced towards the trees, the sound of shouts and voices behind them told them they had been seen. It was Rushton. This was the confrontation she had been dreading.

She crouched over her horse's neck, terrified she would be swept from the saddle by overhanging branches. Entering the trees at this speed was foolhardy, but their lives depended on it. Robert and George were close behind her. She was glad of that.

'Dismount, leave the horses and get behind those trees. I'll take care of this.'

She needed no second urging but flung herself from the saddle and dived into the dense undergrowth that surrounded the trees. She did not stop until she was certain she could not be seen from the road. Her chest was heaving, her mouth dry. From her hiding place she could see nothing, but she could hear and that was bad enough.

★   ★   ★

Robert checked both his pistols were ready to fire and his sword slipped easily from its scabbard. He removed his rifle from its holster on the back of his saddle. The ammunition pouch was in his saddle-bag. He dropped it into his pocket. Leaving Silver with the other two horses he dropped to a crouch and ran through the trees until he was at the far end of the wood. The two coaches were stationary on the road a quarter of a mile away.

Using his spyglass he saw two rough-looking men jump down from the second coach. They were carrying pistols: he had not expected them to be armed with more than cudgels. Then he looked at the elegant man standing beside the first coach, a smaller man at his side. Both gentlemen were also holding weapons. So, that was how it was to be. If they wanted violence, he was the man for the job. This was what he was trained for, had spent all his adult life doing.

Ice cold, ready for battle, he intended to protect his wife and the stable boy. They would not be taken, and he would kill if he had to. His old skills were back. He was up to the task.

He wove in and out of the bushes confident he was unobserved, until he found the vantage point he needed. He dropped to his knees, tipped ball and powder from the pouch, removed the ramrod from the barrel of his rifle. Officers were not usually experts with this weapon, but he had always thought it best to be as good, if not better, than the men he commanded. At one point he had been captain of a band of riflemen, chosen men, skirmishers, the most valuable group in the regiment.

He loaded the gun and waited. Rushton and his companion had seen the horses in the trees, they couldn't see Annabel or the boy, but would guess they were hiding in the dense undergrowth. They would expect him to be hiding with them.

His eyes narrowed, he raised the weapon to his shoulder, they were just out of range, but he would drop them both without compunction if needs be. He turned his gaze to the henchmen who were being directed across the fields towards them. These were paid assassins, there would be no repercussions if they died.

He steadied himself, aimed and fired. The

report echoed in the silence sending birds and small animals rushing for cover. Before the second man could turn and run Robert had reloaded and fired again.

He had not shot to kill, but to disarm and prevent further intervention from these two. The first he had shot through the shoulder, the second through the lower leg. Neither wound would be fatal if attended to properly, but both would leave them *hors de combat*.

The rifle reloaded, he rose smoothly to his feet and strode out into the open. He was well out of pistol range. Rushton must realize and knew he was in mortal danger. He watched as he decided what to do. He strode closer, until he was in hailing distance.

'Rushton, it's over. You will not take Lady Sophia back with you, not now, not ever. Next time I shoot it will be fatal to the person who receives the bullet. Do I make myself quite clear?'

'What the devil do you mean by this, Dudley? You have no right to shoot my retainers. I shall have the law on you for this. Lady Sophia is my property; Miss Bentley also within my control. I have the legal papers here.' He patted his pocket to emphasize his point. 'You must hand them over to me or it will be the worst for you. I shall call out the militia. You will hang for what you have done today.'

'I doubt it. But I'm prepared to take that risk. Your name is infamous throughout Town. You are an evil bastard, and I will pull the trigger without the slightest compunction if you provoke me further.'

He saw the men exchange glances, and the smaller of the two began to edge towards the carriage door. 'Follow your man, Rushton, he has the right idea.'

'I shall not forget this, Dudley, I have a long arm, friends in high places. I shall hunt you down and have you killed.'

Robert's finger began to close. He levelled the barrel and his opponent caved in. Rushton turned and dived into the carriage, the next moment it was thundering away, and the second followed it.

Damn and blast it! He had expected the driver and groom of the second coach to climb down and collect the wounded men. What the devil was he to do with them? He could hardly leave them here to bleed to death.

He shouted to Annabel, 'It's safe to come out, but we have to deal with these wounded men; we cannot leave them here to die.'

The two men were inordinately grateful for his assistance, obviously expecting to be abandoned by him as they had been by their master.

'They was fine shots, sir, never seen better. You could have killed us both stone dead so I much appreciate I'm still alive.'

'Be silent. I might change my mind.'

The man subsided, his friend merely groaned. Annabel produced strips torn from her petticoat and between them they patched their assailants up. He would have to put them on the baggage horse and take them to the nearest hostelry.

'I do not intend to hand these two over to the authorities, we have as much to lose as they do by involving them. We'll dump them somewhere, give them a guinea to pay their way, and then turn back and head for Brandon Hall.'

Annabel seemed unfazed by all the excitement. 'I wonder where Sir Randolph and Hughes have gone. Surely, if we leave the two men on the side of the road, they will return for them in time?'

'They were heading back towards London, why should they return in this direction?'

He glanced over his shoulder to check that the two men could not have been eavesdropping. 'No, we must take them on towards Norwich until we come to some-where we can leave them. Then George must take care of them; I shall give him sufficient to get himself home afterwards.'

'Do you think my stepfather might come back? Must we still use subterfuge to be safe?'

'It does not hurt to be vigilant, my love. He was prepared to kill in order to take you, why else did he have pistols ready? I believe I have scared them off, but I am not taking any chances.' He deliberately did not mention that Rushton intended to call out the militia and have him arrested.

Her face paled. 'In which case, you're right to be cautious. We must set off at once. We must not be overtaken whilst we are trailing along the road with the injured men.'

Fortuitously there was a substantial coaching inn only three miles down the road. He dumped the two men outside and went in to speak to the landlord. The man was quite happy to send for the doctor, and to take care of the injured men until they were well enough to continue on their journey.

Robert was pleased to know that a mail coach was due to call that afternoon and could take George as far as Ipswich. From there he could hire a hack and get himself home. He made a point of saying they were continuing to Norwich, that they must press on as they wished to be there by nightfall.

Annabel remained outside, she had sent George to find himself something to eat. Their horses were tethered to a rail contentedly munching hay. She wandered out to the side of the inn where there was a large duck pond. Robert was taking an unconscionable time sorting out the arrangements. She glanced up; there were dark clouds racing in from the coast, the weather was deteriorating. They were likely to get drenched before they completed their journey tonight.

They were going to Brandon Manor to return the hunter and collect the missing carriage horses. They must let Lady Barton know what had happened to her brother. The sound of carriage wheels alerted her. Her fingers clenched. Her stepfather was more cunning than either of them had supposed. He had turned back immediately and followed them. It was too late to call for help, she must run and hide until Robert returned.

She had taken no more than three paces when she was faced by Hughes, a pistol levelled at her heart. Then her arms were seized by Sir Randolph.

'I have you, Sophia. Where's Annabel? It is her that I have come for.'

She might still have a chance. He had

recognized the riding habit, had not seen *her* since she was a slender girl of fifteen summers.

'You shall not have my daughter, you monster, she is inside with Major Dudley. He will protect her with his life.'

She had pitched her voice to exactly mimic her mother's tones, and he did not question it. He snarled at her and raised his fist. There was a blinding pain and her world went black.

★ ★ ★

Robert was still talking to the landlord when George hurtled through the door. 'He's took her, sir. Come quick, them men are back!'

Robert spun, cursing his inattention, wishing he had his rifle with him, but it was too late for that. He erupted from the door. Two unfortunate guests, who had just alighted from their gig, were so terrified by his fearsome appearance the lady fainted and the gentleman dropped to his knees in terror.

Robert ignored them. Rushton had Annabel in his grip, was twisting her arm and shouting. Her head was low, not looking at him directly. And then her assailant raised his fist and struck her on the temple. She collapsed in a heap of blue velvet to the ground.

His eyes misted with fury. Exploding into action, he drew his sword and charged. He raised his weapon, Rushton stared death in the face. The man stepped back clutching his chest. The blade did not reach its target. To his astonishment Sir Randolph choked and fell backwards as if pole-axed. A slight sound behind him warned him someone else was there. He turned as the other man raised his gun.

The man was not a killer, he hesitated a second too long, giving Robert the advantage. He lunged. His sword spitted his opponent, killing him instantly. Ignoring the shouts and gasps from behind him, he dropped his sword and picked up his wife.

Her head flopped, her face was waxy white. If she was dead, then his own life was as good as over. God — no — not again! His mind spun back to that dreadful day after the Battle of Valencia.

'Colonel, there's a woman wants a word, sir.'

Robert shook his head. 'Not now, Jenkins, tell her to wait. I have urgent matters to attend to here.'

His duties completed, he strode off to return home to his beloved intended, Maria. They were due to be married the following day. She was staying in his house tonight well

278

chaperoned by her duenna. Having her beside him would make the grim realities of war more bearable.

The door to his house was swinging open. He paused. Why wasn't it locked as usual? He withdrew his sword, his heart hammering, and stepped inside. The bolts had been smashed; the house broken in to.

Only then did he recall that a woman had asked to speak to him. He surged forward. 'Maria? Maria, where are you?'

A woman was sobbing above him in a bedchamber. He took the stairs three at a time, bursting in to stop, horror-struck. 'Maria, no, Maria, sweetheart.' He stumbled forward to fall on his knees beside the still form. Her hands were cold, her face grey. She was dead.

Her duenna screamed at him from the other side of the bed, 'It's your fault. I came for you, but you ignored me. My Maria would not have killed herself, condemned her soul to Purgatory, if you had come when I asked. Her blood is on your hands, sênor.'

Maria had taken her own life? He shook his head. 'Why, why did she do it?'

The woman raised her ravaged face. 'Two common soldiers broke in and violated her. I ran to fetch you, but you ignored me. She took the laudanum from my room and swallowed it all. I thought her resting. If you had returned you could have told my angel that you still loved her. She would have got over the shame in time.' The woman's harsh sobbing filled the room.

He couldn't cry. He was frozen. Maria had died because of his inattention. He was to blame. Leaning over, he kissed her icy lips. 'I shall never love again, my darling; I do not deserve to be happy.'

It was happening again. Annabel must not die; he loved her. She had released him from his penance.

20

'That's not Lady Sophia, it's Miss Bentley.'

Robert raised his tearstreaked face to see a youngish woman, dressed in servant's apparel. She was staring down at Annabel in bewilderment.

'No, this is my wife, Mrs Sinclair.' He could think of nothing else to say, his brain refused to work, to accept the fact that he was clutching the mortal remains of the woman he loved to distraction.

A rustle of material and the strange woman knelt beside him. She reached out and rested her fingers on Annabel's neck. 'She has a steady pulse, sir, she's no more than stunned. Your wife is not dead.'

Slowly his world tilted back on course and he regained his equilibrium. He drew a shuddering breath, ignoring his tears. He had been mistaken, she was alive. Thank God for that! He held her close, stroking her face tenderly.

'Shall we get Mrs Sinclair inside, sir? She would be better resting in a chamber until the doctor can see to her.'

Doctor? Yes, had he not been sent for to

attend to the men he'd wounded? Still dazed by what he had so nearly lost, he stood up holding his precious burden close to his heart. The young woman led the way. It was only then he became aware of the small group of spectators who had gathered to watch him kill Annabel's attackers. No doubt he was already a marked man. He had shot two men, butchered another and frightened the fourth to death. Still, he would do it again if anyone threatened his beloved.

The landlord greeted him at the door. 'I have prepared a fresh room for you, sir. Follow me and I'll take you there. I shall send the doctor directly to you when he arrives. He must deal with the other patients after he has seen to Mrs Sinclair.'

The chamber was commodious, but it had no separate parlour. Robert walked across to the bed and laid her down. She was pale, but not as cold as she had been. The livid bruise on her face was the only evidence that she had been injured.

The young woman appeared at his side, a wet cloth in her hand. 'Excuse me, sir, but a cold compress on the injury will lessen the swelling.'

Reluctantly he stepped to one side. 'What's your name? How do you come to know my wife?'

The woman was leaning over Annabel holding the wet cloth against the lump. 'I was travelling in the second coach, sir. I have been working for Sir Randolph in London for many years. I knew Lady Sophia and Miss Bentley . . . I beg your pardon, Mrs Sinclair. I guessed exactly what that monster was planning and volunteered to accompany him, hoping I would have the opportunity to help them escape, if hc did find them.'

He nodded. 'And your name?'

'Theresa, sir.'

'Mrs Sinclair requires a maid. Do you care to take that position?'

'I do indeed, sir, I'm most grateful. If you would care to leave Mrs Sinclair in my care, I reckon there are things you need to do downstairs.'

He stared at the woman in astonishment. Since when had maidservants presumed to give *him* orders? Then he looked down at his hands, they were shaking like a *blanc-manger*. He grinned sheepishly. What he needed was a stiff drink to steady his nerves. He had never been so discommoded in a skirmish before. He had killed dozens of men in his time, wounded hundreds more, the fact that he was in love appeared to be unsettling his system.

'I shall do as you suggest, Theresa.' He

turned at the door. 'However, if you wish to remain in my employ, I suggest that you refrain from giving me instructions.'

He closed the door softly. He could imagine what her expression must be, he was still smiling when he reached the hall. He was finally free of Maria's death, free to love again. He wanted to shake the hand of every man he met.

He headed for the snug and found the landlord conversing happily with the two men he had shot. They were tucking in to meat pasties and downing pots of ale and nodded and smiled at him as if he was an old friend.

The world was becoming more peculiar by the minute. Maidservants giving *him* orders, men he had just shot waving and smiling at him. What next?

'Landlord, I would like a large brandy. Also, I need to speak to the two travellers who arrived when the fracas started. I have to make my apologies to them.'

The landlord hurried over. 'There's no need to do that, sir, they fully understood the urgency. Mr and Mrs Jackson are in a private parlour, to the left of the vestibule. The lady has fully recovered, but I'm sure she will appreciate a visit from yourself. Shall I bring your brandy to you there?'

Robert nodded and retraced his steps. He

was about to knock on the door when it opened and a portly gentleman, in old-fashioned frockcoat, stepped out.

'Colonel Sinclair, at your service, Mr Jackson. I have come to offer my apologies to you and your good wife. And to enquire how she does after her swoon?'

The man offered his hand and Robert took it. The man pumped it up and down as if drawing water. 'There's no need to apologize, my good sir, you're a brave man. We know the full story, and applaud your actions. My wife is fully recovered, there's no need for you to speak to her.'

Robert could see over the older man's shoulder into the room beyond. Mrs Jackson was sitting at a table simpering and smiling at him. Good grief! No, he would far rather not go in to her. She obviously regarded him as some sort of heroic figure.

'In which case, Mr Jackson, if you will excuse me, I have urgent business outside.' This was only a half lie; he did need to check on the horses, to see if George had had the common sense to get them taken care of.

The yard was empty, the horses obviously in the stables. George appeared from round the corner and rushed to greet him. 'I ain't never seen the likes, sir. You did for them two good and proper. How is Mrs . . . er . . . Dudley?'

'Mrs Sinclair has a slight concussion, George, she will be better very soon, I'm sure. I think we had better get this straight. I am Colonel Sinclair, the lady I am travelling with, is my wife. Lady Sophia and Major Dudley are, by now, safely in London I should think.'

'I guessed something of the sort, Colonel. The landlord tells me there's a mail coach calls in here later this afternoon. Did you want me to be on it? I can return easy enough from Ipswich.' The boy eyed him hopefully. 'I could stay on with you. In fact, if you could find a place for me permanent like, I reckon that would suit me a treat.'

'And your parents? Will they not be wanting you to return?'

The lad shook his head vigorously. 'They'll be right pleased to be rid of me, sir, I've never really settled to the quiet life. I was always after a bit of excitement. Cockfighting, prize fights. I was off if I got half the chance and a few pennies to spend.'

Robert groaned inwardly, he was becoming soft in the head. 'Then you may stay with me. You seem to have developed a fondness for Mrs Sinclair's gelding. There are not many grooms who can handle him. But I warn you,

286

I'll have no shenanigans in my employ. Is everything sorted out here?'

'Right and tight, sir. I ain't particular, sir, and I can sleep in a stable if I have to.'

Satisfied that George would take care of his horses he decided to organize the removal of the corpses. It would do no good to the landlord's business to have bodies lying around outside. To his relief this matter had already been dealt with.

He walked over to the two carriages. The coachmen were standing about disconsolately but straightened up on seeing him. God's teeth! Was he to employ these fellows as well? He would require a coach to take them back to Brandon Hall; the second coach could take a message into London and deliver it to Dudley and Lady Sophia.

'You there, I'm prepared to employ you on a temporary basis as I have need of a coach to transport my wife and her maid to Brandon Hall tomorrow.'

The man he addressed grinned toothlessly. His wary expression turned to joy. 'Thank God for that, sir. We was wondering how we was to get on now that the master's dead.'

'We shall not be leaving today, I suggest you get your vehicle off the road and the horses seen to.' The driver hopped back on the coach immediately.

Robert turned to the second vehicle, the one that had contained the two injured men and Theresa. 'I want you to take a letter to Lady Sophia and Major Dudley right away. I'm going in to write the missive. Your beasts ready for another journey?'

The coachman tugged his forelock. 'Thank you, sir, thank you, sir, if we don't push them they'll do fine.'

He turned his back on the men knowing they would scurry to his bidding. He supposed that there would be some relative to claim ownership of Rushton's estate, but until then he would make use of his servants and coaches himself. A gig was approaching, a man of middle years at the reins. Excellent, it must be the doctor.

He waited in the yard until the man tied the reins around the post and jumped down. 'Good afternoon, I am Colonel Sinclair, you have several patients to see and two death certificates to write out.'

The man seemed a little taken aback by his abrupt greeting. He was above average height, with florid complexion, a bald pate and grey whiskers. 'I am indeed the doctor, sir. Smithson at your service. I received a summons to attend two men who had been shot, I had no notion there were others to see.'

'My wife has a head injury — she's upstairs — I wish you to see her first. Then there are the two men with bullet wounds, if you can patch them up, I wish them to return to London today.'

'Are the two cadavers a part of this as well?'

'They are, sir. One body is down to me, the other to the Lord Almighty.'

Robert was tired of all this question and answer, he wanted the man upstairs with Annabel, wanted to be certain she was not seriously hurt. He strode through the hostelry and up to the room. Inside, the curtains had been drawn around the bed. He couldn't see if she was conscious.

'Is that you, my love? I am so glad, I have a shocking headache, Theresa tells me there are bodies everywhere.'

Delighted to hear her voice, he bounded to the bed snatching the curtains back to smile down at her dear face. 'I see you have no need for the doctor, my darling, but he's here anyway, so be quiet and let him examine you.'

She pulled a face and his heart flipped. He stood to one side whilst Smithson checked her over. The doctor stood back, a satisfied smile on his face.

'No need for my interference, sir. Your wife has a nasty bruise, but she has suffered no lasting harm. You can resume your journey whenever you wish.'

Robert grinned and shook the doctor's hand. 'Excellent, now I shall have you taken down to your other patients.' He beckoned to the maid standing at the far side of the room viewing him with distinct wariness. 'Theresa, take Dr Smithson down to deal with the men in the snug. Then have the landlord take him to see the bodies.' He smiled wryly. 'As you appear so knowledgeable, I shall leave you to explain to the doctor what took place today.'

The woman curtsied nervously. 'Yes, sir, I shall do so at once. And I beg your pardon for speaking out of turn earlier.'

He smiled and she looked relieved. 'I shall not be needing you here, make yourself useful cleaning and pressing our clothes.'

She snatched up the three bags and almost ran from the room.

★ ★ ★

Annabel watched this exchange with amusement. She had tried to explain to Theresa that her husband might appear fearsome but underneath he was the kindest and most understanding of men. In time they would deal famously together.

The door closed and there was an unmistakable sound of the bolt being pushed across. A wave of fear engulfed her; he had promised nothing intimate would take place between them. He could not have changed his mind so soon.

Then she saw his expression, his face gentle, his eyes glowing with love.

'My darling, I cannot tell you how I felt when I saw you crumpled on the ground. I know we married in haste, but I want you to know that it is not a marriage of convenience for me. I love you. I thought never to say this to another woman again, but I love you and pray that in time you will come to feel the same.'

She stared at him, unable to take in what he had said. He loved her? Smiling, she held out her hand to him. 'I have loved you this age. However, things happened in my past that have made me wary of intimacy.'

He dropped on to the bed taking both her hands. 'I don't expect you to do anything you don't want, my love. I'm in no hurry. As you learn to trust me, to be comfortable around me, you will feel differently, I promise you. But I tell you this, even if we never consummate our marriage, I shall still love you, never be unfaithful, and be content. As long as you are next to me, knowing I can wake up and fall asleep with you breathing beside me, that shall be enough for me.'

She reached out to stroke his bristle-roughened cheek. He leant his face against her hand. There was no need for words, his eyes said everything. 'You look so tired, my love, why don't you take off your boots and outer garments and sleep beside me? Neither of us had much rest last night, the last two days have been so frenetic we are quite exhausted.'

He carried her fingers to his mouth, kissing each one in turn then lowered his head. His lips trailed tenderly from the corner of her mouth, down her neck and back again. She was melting inside and her hands slid round his neck of their own volition.

'You make me feel so strange. I don't understand what happens to me when you're this close.'

'I want to touch every inch of you, my darling. But if I do not stop right now, I shall find it difficult not to take things too far.'

She gazed up at his face, deep into his eyes, then drew him down and kissed him. She loved the feel of his lips on the hers. Then she pushed him away gently.

'Come to bed, Robert, I would like to fall asleep in your arms. I owe you my life and my mother has been set free. We have the rest of our lives to get to know each other.'

'There's a secret in my past I must tell you.

Promise me you will not interrupt until you have heard the whole. If, after hearing this sorry tale, you no longer wish to be my wife I shall release you.'

'Tell me quickly, and then I shall tell you my nightmare and we can start afresh together.'

He stumbled through his story and her heart broke for his suffering. 'Robert, how awful. It's small wonder you were reluctant to become involved again. What happened to your first love was not your fault; you must put it behind you. I love you. I don't blame you and you must no longer blame yourself.'

'My darling, I can't believe it's over.'

Her toes curled at the intensity of his look. 'I must tell you . . . '

'No, you must not. I know Rushton frightened you and that he mistreated your mother. Do not think of it again, my darling.'

He stood and turning his back removed his blood-spattered jacket and grimy shirt, then hooked his boots off using the fender to help him. His stockings and britches followed. At that point she thought it better to close her eyes.

A few moments later the bed dipped, but instead of feeling naked flesh against her, he climbed in on top of the linen sheet and then rolled to her side.

'I love you, Annabel Sinclair, and I'm going to make you the happiest woman on God's earth however long it takes.'

She snuggled up against him, resting her damaged head against his naked chest, his arm encircled her. She felt protected, loved — safe for the first time in her life.

When Annabel woke, the room was dark, lit only by the flicker of coal light. She needed the commode, urgently. He was still breathing evenly beside her. Carefully she removed his arm, slipped out of bed and found what she required behind the screen. From the mantelshelf she removed a candlestick and pushed the wick into the flames. Holding this she crept across to the window and closed the shutters. The yard was quiet, it must be the middle of the night.

She was no longer tired, had been asleep too long already. But she was extremely hungry. The candle hovered above her husband. He looked younger when he was sleeping, the lines smoothed out, his face relaxed. She put a tentative finger out and traced the line of his thick eyebrows, pushing a lock of hair from his forehead.

His hand shot out and trapped her. Startled, she squeaked and dropped the candlestick on her foot.

'Ouch! That hurt. What is it about you,

Sinclair, that causes me to be injured whenever I'm in your vicinity?'

There was a gentle pull, when she was close enough a second hand reached out and grabbed her waist. She was tumbled into bed to lie almost on top of his naked frame. His fingers reached out to her braid.

'I want to see your hair loose, my love. I was dreaming about it, remembering the first time I saw you. Sit up, sweetheart, let me do it for you.'

She wasn't sure this was sensible, his touch was sending shockwaves through her body, her very core was glowing like the embers in the fire. What was happening to her? Why did his touch make her feel light-headed? Why was the blood pulsing around her body as if she had been running in a race? Then her hair was loose. He buried his fingers in it, then his hands drew her closer, closer, until his lips found hers and she forgot everything apart from the magic he was weaving around her.

21

Robert wanted to make love to his wife, she was pliant in his arms, pressing her body against his making him lose control.

'Darling, I'm not going to break my word. You're my life now. When I make love to you for the first time I want you to feel the same way as I do.'

Reluctantly he rolled over, taking her with him until she was safely on her side of the bed. He pulled the covers over her and kissed her again. 'There, sweetheart. You must go back to sleep. No, don't touch me, I shall be unable to restrain myself if you do.'

'Thank you, Robert. I was feeling most peculiar, your touch has the most unusual effect on my senses.' The bed moved and she scrambled out again.

'Annabel, what now?'

'I'm wide awake. I'm going to light the candles. If I remain over here, is that far enough for you? I wish we had something to eat, Robert, I am decidedly hungry.'

'Don't think about it, my love, the kitchen is closed. We shall spend the time in conversation. We have much to discuss.'

The room was fully illuminated, her hair floating around her like golden silk. He must think of something else or he would go mad. She must remain out of arm's reach. 'I didn't tell you, sweetheart, I sent a letter to your mother and the major about what took place here today. It went with the second coach.'

Her smile made his heart somersault. 'That's wonderful. With luck they will still be at the inn. Did you suggest they return to Brandon Hall?'

'I did, my darling. You shall be reunited with your mama tomorrow.'

★ ★ ★

She settled comfortably in an armchair, tucking her feet under her. 'I thought we were to go abroad, to Italy? But I would much rather be at Brandon with . . . ' She hesitated, embarrassed he might think she preferred her mother's company to his. That was not the case, but she would be happy to remain at Brandon Hall indefinitely.

'Until we know each other better, I think we should remain where you are most comfortable.'

Her eyes pricked. He looked so sad, she could not bear to think it was *she* who made him so dejected. Why was she feeling this way? Why wasn't she thrilled to be returning to her mama? It was too late to retract her remark. It would be safer to talk of something else.

'Robert, I think that my mama and your major have formed an attachment. Do you think they will get married now that she's free?'

'I'm certain of it. Why should they wait for the required period of mourning? They have spent the past few nights closeted together, in the eyes of the world Lady Sophia is already his mistress.'

'Both of us married, and to gentlemen we only met two weeks ago! The vicar must be called, not only to perform the ceremony but to bury Great-aunt Beth in the churchyard. I'm so happy, everything has worked out perfectly.'

His expression made something burst within her. 'All our lives have been turned upside down. We will no longer be associated in any way with the name Rushton.' Her stomach gurgled loudly. 'I'm going to the kitchen to find food, I cannot possibly wait until morning. I'm quite faint with hunger.' He chuckled and looked rather pointedly at her *déshabillé*. 'You're quite right, I cannot parade around in public like this.' She smiled. 'Robert, it would not take a moment for you to dress. No one would think twice about meeting a gentleman downstairs. I'm sure you could discover some sustenance.'

He looked sceptical. She must convince him; she ran across the room and scrambled on to the bed to make her plea more personal. 'Dearest Robert, please consider going down. Even bread and cheese would be wonderful.'

He was propped against the bed head with eyes closed, his naked shoulders gleaming white in the candlelight. All thoughts of food vanished to be replaced by a different kind of hunger. He was so beautiful. His muscles bunched as she watched. She had to touch him, put her fingers on the dark hair that curled across his chest. Without thinking she stretched over. It was springy, quite different from the soft hair on his head.

'Darling girl, please desist. I am only human, I don't know how long I can hold out.'

How curious! A delicious warmth was spreading like fire around her body. If she didn't move she would be committed. She closed her eyes, waiting for the dark image that had haunted her for so long to invade her head. Instead of fear she felt a rush of love for this man who was not a stranger any more but her dear husband.

'My love, I want to be your true wife. I don't wish to wait.'

For a second he didn't react, then his eyes blazed, but this time she didn't recoil. 'Darling, are you quite sure? I love you so much, want to bury myself inside you, make you mine for ever. Once this begins I doubt I shall be able to stop, I need you too much. It's killing me, holding back from you like this.'

'Show me how to love you properly. I want to share everything with you.'

His arms closed around her waist and she fell on to his chest. For several, breathless intoxicating minutes he kissed her until she burned for something more. She wanted to feel her skin against his, her nightgown was no longer needed.

'Robert, I am too hot.'

He did not need telling twice. With gentle hands he gripped her gown and pulled it over her head. 'Come closer, sweetheart, let me feel your skin touching mine. Let me make love to you.' And he did.

We do hope that you have enjoyed reading this large print book.

Did you know that all of our titles are available for purchase?

We publish a wide range of high quality large print books including:
Romances, Mysteries, Classics
General Fiction
Non Fiction and Westerns

Special interest titles available in large print are:
The Little Oxford Dictionary
Music Book
Song Book
Hymn Book
Service Book

Also available from us courtesy of Oxford University Press:
Young Readers' Dictionary
(large print edition)
Young Readers' Thesaurus
(large print edition)

For further information or a free brochure, please contact us at:
Ulverscroft Large Print Books Ltd.,
The Green, Bradgate Road, Anstey,
Leicester, LE7 7FU, England.
Tel: (00 44) **0116 236 4325**
Fax: (00 44) **0116 234 0205**

THE GHOSTS OF NEDDINGFIELD HALL

Fenella-Jane Miller

When Miss Culley and her entire staff vanish without trace from Neddingfield Hall, Hester Frobisher believes she alone can solve the mystery and find her great-aunt. However, she's obliged to accept help from her cousin Ralph, the Earl of Waverley. Ralph, a formidable veteran of the Peninsular Wars, convinces Hester that they can make an invincible team. But sinister forces are at work to lure the two, and those around them, towards their deaths. No one at Neddingfield is safe. There's something seeking to destroy them. Is it ghosts? Can Hester's quick wits and Ralph's courage save them all?

THE HOUSE PARTY

Fenella-Jane Miller

When Lady Dalrymple, Penelope Coombs' great-aunt, accepts an invitation to Lord Edward Weston's house party, Penny is displeased: slighted by the Earl of Rushford during her season she has no wish to repeat the experience. Lord Weston secretly works for the British government and is searching for the traitor who is smuggling gold to France. Suspecting the pilot of a travelling air balloon party, Edward invites the balloonists to his home to investigate matters. During a series of alarming events James Weston, Edward's cousin, offers Penny comfort . . . Will the Frenchman, Count Everex, evade capture — can he succeed in his nefarious plans?

A DEBT OF HONOUR

Fenella-Jane Miller

Eliza Fox, devastated by the deaths of her father and fiance, recovers by assuming control of the family estate, firmly believing matrimony has no place in her life. Then Lord Wydale, a notorious rakehell, wins Grove House from her brother, Edmund Fox, who returns to Eliza in the hope that she can save their home. Meanwhile, Mr Fletcher Reed meets Eliza who steals his heart and appears to return his feelings. But can Eliza save her sister and herself from Lord Wydale — and will Fletcher be able to rescue them from the villain?